Portrait of Murder

Rob Riley

Orange Hat Publishing
www.orangehatpublishing.com - Milwaukee, WI

Published by Orange Hat Publishing 2012

ISBN 978-1-937165-10-9

Copyrighted © 2012 by Rob Riley
All Rights Reserved

Printed in the United States of America

This publication and all contents within may not be reproduced or transmitted in any part or in its entirety without the written permission of the author.

This is a work of fiction. The names, places, characters, and incidents are products of the writer's imagination and are not real. Any resemblance to persons, living or dead, actual events, locale, or organizations is purely coincidental.

Orange Hat Publishing would like to express our gratitude to John Konecny for creating the cover design. Also, thanks to Mary Lynne Riley, who provided the inspiring ideas for the cover design.

www.orangehatpublishing.com

Acknowledgement

I wish to thank my wife, Mary Lynne, for her loving support, inspiration, and contributions to my efforts in becoming an author. I would also like to mention the late John Tigges: an author, my mentor, my friend. Without his tutelage, this book would never have been written.

CHAPTER ONE

At noon, sunlight shone through my kitchen window and fell in a wide streak across the kitchen table. Slouching in my chair, I lazily traced my fingertips along the sunlight's path on the corner of the tabletop. I'd just hung up the phone with my friend L.C. Veasley, who'd called me with a disturbing request – could I look for his missing crackhead sister, Roniece? He claimed she'd recently cleaned up, but that she hadn't been seen in five days. I should have told him the truth right away – pipe hitters can't stay clean, and I no longer investigated missing drug addicts. Too often it's a waste of time and money.

But it was L.C., and I'd have done anything to help him out.

I told him to call me back with some information I'd need to get started. I was already growing impatient. My kitchen was my office, and I didn't like hanging around the office any longer than I had to. I was dressed in my standard private detective garb – a red T-shirt and blue jeans – and ready to go. My cell phone finally rang and I picked it up from among the clutter of pencils and papers and a half-empty, blue polished stoneware coffee cup with *I Don't Need No Stinking Badge* stenciled in white letters on the side, all sprawled on the large wood farmhouse table. Among the debris sat a spiffy computer with all the attending gadgets.

Of course, my business card holder, with *Jack Blanchard, Private Investigator* engraved on a tarnished brass plate, sat empty. That's what happens with a guy like me and no secretary.

The caller ID showed L.C.'s name and phone number and I answered the phone with a bored-sounding, "Yeah."

"You ready, Jack?" He had a forceful, deep voice. "You got a pencil and paper?"

I moved aside the coffee cup and grabbed a pencil and Post-It notepad. "Go."

"I want you to talk to a guy, a little prick sittin' in the joint." He sounded edgier than the first time he called.

I stuck the pencil point onto the notepad and waited. "And the little prick's name is . . . ?"

"Yeah. Reggie Thackery. He's doin' seven-to-ten up in Waupun for a drug war killing. Not a bad ride, considering he dinged two people. Been there 'bout a year-and-a half."

I wrote Reggie Thackery's name, then quickly put my pencil down. "And he can help me *how*?"

"It's all I got, brother. He and Roniece were crack asses together, going back years. Sold dope together. He knows as much about her as anybody I know of."

"Until a year-and-a-half ago." I sat back and looked at the sun streak highlighting the mess and office equipment on the table. L.C. was like everyone else – he expected me to turn water into wine.

He continued his description of Reggie Thackery – a nobody, a grease spot who'd been scraped off the inner city streets of Milwaukee and sent to one of two certain destinies for too many young African American males – prison. He was lucky, this time avoiding the alternative – a grave.

I feigned interest. "How'd you decide he could help?"

"Word is he and Roniece were back and forth on the street until he went to jail. They hung out when he lived on the same block as us, back in the day. I was long gone, but Roniece, she always leaned bad, and Thackery, he had dope and guns and everything, even as a teenager."

"So, he's your only notion. I'll start with him. Anything else?" I tried not to sound discouraging.

"The police already checked for Roniece. They don't try too hard with missing adults, and no signs of foul play."

"I was just going to ask about the police." Actually, I hadn't thought of asking about the police. The case felt hopeless, and I was having a hard time ginning up interest enough for even the basics. "Do they know of her drug problem?"

"I mentioned it. She's got a record, so they'll know about it on their own."

I grabbed my coffee cup and swirled the remaining cold, black liquid. I thought of taking a drink, then thought better of it. L.C.'s measured breaths blew into my earpiece. Neither of us spoke for a long moment. I had that door-slamming feeling I always get when I decide that I'm not going to take someone's case. But I wouldn't be doing that to L.C. We went back a long way. I'd check every possibility, even if it meant going through the motions and ending with squat.

"So, the name's Reggie Thackery," I finally said. "Anything else, before I run him on the computer?"

"Only thing would be that Reggie was always crazy, but I heard he really went off the deep end in prison."

He paused, as though expecting me to respond. I said nothing. Reggie's deep-end dive in prison was irrelevant to a going-nowhere, missing-crackhead investigation.

"They said he had visions and shit," L.C. said. "Talks all about shootings and murders, like he sees 'em in his head as he says it. He put a tattoo on his arm. 'Four Dead,' it says."

Interesting, but not exciting. "Four Dead?"

"That's what my guy tells me."

I smiled and propped one leg on the chair next to me. "And your 'guy' is?"

"My *guy*. You know."

L.C. Veasley was a 48-year-old African American survivor of the hardest, meanest streets in Milwaukee's inner city. He'd beat the odds, ditched his disaffection, and become a well-known success story by rehabbing inner city properties. But reflex paranoia still played a role with him. Any time a hipster like L.C. referred to someone as "my guy," you weren't going to get a name.

He continued. "Reggie only calls himself 'Four Dead,' now. Goes wild if anyone calls him by his real name."

It started sounding like an outline of an Edgar Allan Poe story.

"I'm surprised he's still alive," I said. "*Four Dead*. I'm glad I know how to address him."

"You call him 'Four Dead' all you want," L.C., said, raising his voice. "I don't cater to no crazy man's bullshit. He's *Reggie*, to me."

I was hungry. I dropped my foot to the floor, put on the cell phone headset and went to the refrigerator to fix myself a ham and cheese sandwich. L.C. continued talking. *Reggie* was in his early twenties. *Reggie* spent most of his time in the hole. I grabbed my cup from the table, dumped the cold coffee into the sink and poured a fresh cup from the carafe sitting on the kitchen counter, and sat back down in my chair.

I chewed my food and sipped my coffee. I didn't like the way L.C. was piecemealing his information. I operated like a psychiatrist – I needed my clients to tell me everything up front before I could figure a solution. But I didn't push it.

"And I hear the other inmates call Reggie 'Four D,' to piss him off," L.C. said.

"Must be one of those prison things," I said absently. "They get to kill him if he starts a fight over it. That way there's always something for them to look forward to." I finished my lunch and began cleaning up, sweeping breadcrumbs from the table and rinsing my coffee cup before placing it in the sink.

He chuckled dryly. "Better hurry up and talk to him before he's just a puff of smoke."

I assured him I was speeding off, and we hung up. A quick phone call to the Waupun State Prison, 70 miles north of the city, got me a 3:00 p.m. appointment to interview Reggie Thackery, also known as Four Dead. Jesus. I was not enthused. My starting point in finding a missing crackhead was a crazy convict, whom everyone hated and probably all would be happy to kill. And if I were successful, I'd find a hollowed out human being who'd likely be better off if she were dead.

CHAPTER TWO

After the hour-long drive to the prison – an old, gray brick building with high walls surrounding the grounds and steel coils of razor barbs stretched along the top of the walls, glistening beneath an azure sky – I parked my car and went to the prison's main entrance. A two-story turret tower stood about 20 yards to my left. I looked up and imagined a uniformed prison guard with a high-powered rifle standing on the top floor beneath an octagonal roof, watching my every step. That would have been the scene ages ago. One of the ubiquitous modern era security cameras had long since taken his place. I'd been at the prison countless times since I'd begun in law enforcement as a City of Milwaukee cop 24 years earlier, the last nine of which I'd worked as a detective. The place still seemed as ominous as the first time I visited, still emitting a dangerous chill.

Inside the front door, I stood in a vestibule with my arms stretched over my head and my feet spread apart, while Jen Clarke, a middle-aged female guard wearing a midnight blue, tight-fitting uniform whisked over me with a metal detecting wand.

"Hi, Jack," she said, her smile bright and genuine. She had clear white skin and chubby cheeks, gray eyes, short salt-and-pepper hair, a large bosom and a thick middle distorting what once had been a voluptuous body. She was still a looker, in a farmer's wife sort of way.

"Hi Jen," I said, handing her cup of coffee as I walked through the second, overarching metal detector when she was done. "That feels better every time you do it." I'd known her for years and always brought her coffee when I came in the morning.

"Tell me about it."

A short while later I was in the prison visiting section sitting on a cold concrete stool between concrete walls that weren't much wider than my shoulders. The stool, walls and floor were all freshly painted gray. Staring at me through a bulletproof Plexiglas window when I arrived was the young black man who called himself 'Four Dead.'

"Jack Blanchard," he said to me. The circular microphone built into the glass made his voice sound tinny. "They tol' me who you was. You don' look like no dick."

I watched and listened to him closely. He seemed reasonably intelligent, but deeply disturbed, as one would expect of a murderer and a "crazy man," as L.C. had called him. Maybe Four Dead had been expecting someone in a cheap, rumpled suit with a clip-on tie. I'd put on a lightweight, blue denim Harley-Davidson jacket over my T-shirt and blue jeans. I also wore the moderately weathered face of a white man in his 40's, which looked somewhat older with graying hair on top.

"You don' impress me, dick."

He had nerve. He couldn't have been more than five-foot-six, skinny as a rat's tail. A sneeze in the next room would knock him over. His bug-eyed, narrow face was bony and sick looking. His hair was long and bushy and unevenly cut. He reminded me of a scarecrow.

"I'm not here to impress you, Mr. Thackery," I said. "I'm here to interview you." I wanted to see how he'd react to being addressed by his real name.

His bug eyes bugged out even more. He half stood and leaned his face close to the Plexiglas. "You call me 'Four Dead,' bitch," he snarled. He pulled up the left sleeve of his gray jumpsuit and showed me a "4 Dead" tattoo etched in black letters on his scrawny bicep.

He was a sure bet for blowing his stack. And, sure enough, he had changed his name to

"Four Dead."

Something had impressed him deeply for him to carve a bizarre name like that on his own skin. It was a prison tattoo that looked like something an untalented eight-year-old might do. I briefly imagined his unsteady hand scratching the letters onto his arm. He yanked the sleeve back down and plunked himself down hard on his stool, his flinty stare boring holes through me.

"L.C. Veasley sent me," I said. "You know, Roniece Veasley's big brother? Roniece is missing, and he thinks you might have street connections that could help me find her. He also said everyone here in the box calls you 'Four D.' Is it all right if I call you 'Four D'?"

I was leaning hard on his buttons. He had a lot them, all going off at once. But his head was in a nut bag, and guys like that need prodding.

"L.C. cool. He can call me what he want."

He surprised me. The hatred left his eyes. He spoke respectfully. If anything, he looked scared. That didn't surprise me – L.C. could scare respect into anybody. He'd spent his own time in this same prison a couple decades before, and he was still connected to the inside. He always let me know that, what with his "guys," and all.

I forced a broad smile, trying to appear overly enthused. "Okay, then 'Four D' it is. Maybe between you and me and L.C., we can solve this case."

Playing simple sometimes works with a pompous flake with a hair-trigger temper. Four Dead was all of that, and if he thought he had the upper hand, he might be chattier. But he'd shown himself to be unpredictable, and I had to be careful. PIs have different rules than cops. You can't just walk away if a guy gets weird. You have to be patient and follow every rabbit down every hole. The private sector expects results.

He rolled his eyes and snorted. He looked at me as though I were an idiot. It was the best start I could hope for.

"Well, we're off to a good start," I said, maintaining my silly smile. "Maybe we can discuss—"

"I'll talk to you 'cuz of L.C. But we ain't off to no good start. I don' like you."

I dropped my smile and tried to look hurt. "I'm sorry if I offended you. I'm just trying to help L.C. He's worried about his poor kid sister."

"I'd be worried she dead."

I was taken aback, but didn't show it. "Really? Why?"

He had gradually sat forward, leaning his elbows on the ledge before him. Suddenly, he snapped backward, his eyes glazing over, his skin growing a shade lighter. Being a disturbed human being must have aced whatever brainpower he had. He'd surrendered any advantage he may have had, and he'd left himself no choice but to continue talking. He knew that if he stomped off without explaining himself, he'd bring on L.C.'s wrath.

"L.C.'s sister a crazy bitch," he said. "Any time she missing, I figure she dead."

"Why do you figure that?"

"She got trouble with the dope man."

That was important information, the kind not likely to have been given by someone like Four Dead to someone like me. L.C. must have been even scarier than I'd thought.

"So, you'd be worried she's dead," I said. "You think the dope man killed her?"

"All dope mens kills their bitches when they fuck up too much. Or at least, they run 'em off."

I leaned forward, resting my elbows on the ledge before me. "Who is the dope man? And how did Roniece fuck up?"

"Might be two dope mens. And all bitches always fuck up."

"*Two* dope men," I said. "My goodness. You sure it wasn't three, or maybe four?"

He didn't respond, seemed instead to be pulling back once again. But for some reason he couldn't keep his mouth shut, he was volunteering way too much for his own good. I wondered why.

After a long pause he looked at me again and made a broad, fake smile, and held up two fingers. "Two dope mens, and she know too much. She been paranoid like a motherfucker for a long time."

He'd leaned forward to the ledge again. We were nose to nose. I was glad there was a thick window between us. I didn't have a clue as to what motivated him. But, fear of L.C. or not, he was bound to stop giving straight answers eventually, or forget himself and clam up altogether.

"How do you know what she knows? You've been in here a long time."

"I gots m' ways."

L.C.'s instincts had been right. Maybe he'd known even more than he told me.

"Okay," I said, "but what does she know that could give her trouble, or get herself killed?"

"Can't go there."

Maybe he'd started getting lockjaw. "Why?"

"One a' the dope mens is dead. The other dope man's still aroun', a stone fuckin' killer."

Maybe he wasn't getting lockjaw.

These were completely unexpected claims. Roniece's drug involvement had been well known by L.C., but he hadn't mentioned her being involved enough to end up murdered. The possibility of her crawling off to die like a sick animal had gone without saying. Then again, Four Dead was a criminal as well as a screwball, which by definition made him unreliable. Maybe his talk was all drama and Roniece was just burning the crack pipe at both ends, living in a sewer somewhere. At least, he was making things more interesting.

I leaned away and sat straight. "How would any of this affect you?"

He grunted and also sat back. "It don'. Not directly. 'Specially since I don' know the killer dude, and my ass is banked in here. But talkin' 'bout things like *dat* ain' healthy."

"How so?" It was a silly question – guys in prison get killed just for laughs, much less for talking about business in the 'hood. But some things he just wasn't going to volunteer.

He laughed a forced, sarcastic laugh. "Works up my nerves. Gots to double my pills."

Shit. "Your pills?"

He smiled, this time a broad, almost proud smile. "I be a schizo-*phraniac*." He laughed again.

"You mean, schizo-*phrenic*?"

"Uh-uh. Dat the way you white eyes say it."

No wonder he talked so much. A schizophrenic's mind is like Swiss cheese. Unexpected things constantly squirt through the holes, sometimes out their mouths. Trouble was – was it real, or was it mind mush?

He began twitching, tapping his feet, rubbing his chest and arms.

His eyes shifted rapidly while he looked around. The interview was being watched on closed circuit TV and I was afraid he wouldn't have long before they'd drag him back and chain him to a wall, or whatever they do in prison with schizophrenics when they get squirrelly.

What he'd said was plausible, but I wanted to be sure it was real. If there were any possibility that Roniece had had trouble with a killer dope man, the police would have to get involved, pronto.

"L.C. ain't gonna be satisfied with the bullshit you're shoveling. He can reach out and touch you in here. You know that."

Four Dead stopped his twitching and looked at me. "You workin' for L.C., an' nobody else, right?"

"Right."

"He'll kick your punk ass too, you go tellin' the wrong people."

"I know that." I put a worried look on my face. "He'd hurt me in a heartbeat."

Four Dead took a deep breath, sat forward and leaned on the ledge again, resigned to telling me the story. Or, *a* story. I braced myself. He wouldn't be too generous with what he could recall if he were scared, or maybe even snitching on himself.

"So, lay it on me," I said, once again leaning as close to the window as I could.

He sighed and turned his head away. He looked back to me. "It ain' gonna be easy, talkin' wid you."

"I know. I'm not hip. But we ain't in the street, and I ain't slick like you. So, lay it on me."

He sighed again, this time sounding resigned. "Roniece a dope runner. She got crack and money from her guy, so she didn' have to be no 'ho. She bring me in, and I serves at some dope houses, and deals a little for m'self. The dope man was big time. Earl Jones – that his name."

"I assume he's the dead dope man?"

"Yup. Roniece know his girlfriend Kim since they was kids. I think Kim the one who hook Roniece up wid' him, an' dat's why she get a piece a' the party, 'stead of havin' to *be* the party, like a ho." He paused to laugh at his own joke. "Couple years ago the dope man an' Kimmy, they gets shot in a alley in his car, along wid two other dudes. They was all killed."

Four in one blow? What a coincidence, Four Dead. My heart beat faster. I didn't remember the case. The city had so many multiple drug murders, they all blended together.

"Was it ever solved?" I asked.

"No. Everybody know another dealer did it, but no one know who."

"The stone fuckin' killer, you mean. He was the other dope dealer."

"Right."

"And you think Roniece knows something about it?"

"Maybe. She all hooked up. I know after the killin' she scared, but she never talk 'bout it. I don't know nuthin' more."

He was holding back – lying "like a motherfucker," as he would put it. "Did the police talk to Roniece about the murders?"

"Don' know."

"Is there anything else?"

"Naw, man. I don' know nuthin' more."

I relaxed, turned my head to the side, and took a moment to think things through. Four Dead couldn't have learned all he claimed to know about the homicide from a terrified Roniece Veasley. Street dudes often nickname themselves after what they believe to be their personal attributes – sometimes after an event they've been involved with. The 4 Dead carving on his arm couldn't have been a stronger indication of the latter. I had no way of guessing how much Roniece actually knew about the killings, if anything.

L.C. hadn't told me anything about Four Dead's own murder case, except, of course, that he'd been in prison a year-and-a-half for the crime. Maybe it took six months from his arrest to his trial, and he was sentenced to prison a year-and-a-half ago. That would coincide with the Jones multiple murder. It seemed to me there was an almost certain link between Four Dead's caper and the four who'd been shot dead in the alley. And Four Dead had mentioned Roniece being in danger for a reason, whatever that was. The possibility grew in my mind that Roniece could be more than a simple missing person.

Four Dead's nickname being a sore spot with him, I wanted to ask him more about it, but at the right time. I turned my head to look at him. "So, when did you get popped for murder?"

His ready, cynical laugh erupted again. "Two weeks after Earl Jones an' all dem."

Just as I'd figured. I sat on the edge of my stool and leaned forward again. "What does your new name and that tattoo on your arm have to do with Jones's and the others' murders?"

I expected his temper to blow, but he surprised me again. His eyes widened, his color deepened and a smile stretched across his face.

"It got nothin' to do with it." He laughed loudly once again, making a prolonged giggle while he leaned over the ledge and rolled his forehead from side to side on his outstretched arm. He seemed to be relishing some private joke.

I waited. He sat up, continued grinning, and stared off. He apparently needed constant reminding of L.C.'s power to reach inside and squeeze him, to keep telling the truth. But I decided to wait.

I sat forward even more. "What's the story on *your* murder rap?"

For a long moment he didn't respond. He sat slumped, his back and shoulders rounded off, and finally looked at me. "Some dudes thought I had somethin' to do with Earl Jones's murder. Comes after me, I shoots 'em. Self defense, but I got jammed for murder, 'cuz the community's tired of all the drug wars."

I placed my lips close to the microphone, almost mashing my face against the Plexiglas. I deeply arched my brow for effect. "Why would anyone think you had something to do with Jones's murder? You sold drugs for him. You were on his side. Right?"

"Thought I went renegade, or somethin'."

"That happened two weeks after the Earl Jones's killing. But, in the meantime, Roniece somehow knows too much, gets scared and reports back to you. Is that it?" I put a hard edge on every word, steadily raising my voice.

His eyes had gone dull, half hooded. He looked down and away. I let his lies and half-truths drift away on the hot air that blew them. I had to steer him back to the reason I was there.

"So, Four Dead, how can I find Roniece?" I asked, softening my tone a little.

He looked up, straightened his back and squared his shoulders.

His face became an image of defiance. "How the fuck would I know?"

I leaned back a little. "Her background, I mean. Who are her friends – her boyfriend would be nice – and where does she hang out? L.C. knows she has a whole life he knows nothing about." I varied the tone of my voice, making it sing-song, almost reverting back to my earlier, simpleton mode.

"Don' know no boyfriend. She gots a auntie, or something. She go to her when she wanna disappear. Don' know if she still do."

"Good. And her auntie's name?"

"Don' know. Don' know where she live."

Another fat lie. I dropped the simpleton act once again. "I don't believe that," I said sharply. "Why won't you give it up?"

"Don't remember her name. And she move since I been in here."

"How do you know she moved?"

He looked exasperated. "It's what I hear. I don' know nothin' more."

I was getting frustrated. "How about places Roniece hangs around, things she does? You know – does she collect money for the United Way?"

A disbelieving look crossed his face. "Think I'm done talkin'." His expression changed to one of disgust while he spoke.

"L.C. isn't done. Remember?"

He sucked in and blew out a short breath. "She hang around a bar on J Street. Don' know the name."

I'd grown tired of him. Despite his fear of L.C., his haywire brain kept him too scattered, and me too off stride. But L.C. would certainly be interested in what he'd said, even if it was mostly bullshit. Even if the cops had already investigated everything about Roniece's missing case – and I was sure they hadn't – I figured I'd have better luck.

It was time to go. If he thought it necessary, L.C. would have a prison insider put Four Dead's nuts in a grinder and get more out of him.

I stood. "Well, Mr. Four Dead, it's been a slice of heaven. But I've got things to do."

He didn't reply. The same dull look as before crossed his face, with his eyelids stretching over his bug eyes. He looked drained of energy, as though he hadn't heard me. Must have been the side effect of his medication. Schizophrenics take lots of it – especially when they're in custody and forced to take it. On their own, they stop, and go stark raving mad. I wondered how long it had been since he'd acted up in prison. That would tell the story about his meds.

He was one messed-up guy. I turned and walked away. I almost felt sorry for him.

CHAPTER THREE

After leaving the prison I drove back to town, directly to L.C.'s house. He lived in the heart of the inner city, in a large Victorian-style home that had been built in the early twentieth century. He'd completely remodeled it himself. The house was one of only a few left in random locations on the block. His block had become what the locals called a "gap tooth," with at least half of the homes having either burned down or been razed. Some that still stood were vacant, and some of those were used as drug houses. They, too, frequently were burned down, courtesy of the drug wars.

L.C. let me in through the side door, and we sat at his kitchen table. He wasn't happy when I told him what Four Dead had said.

"I heard about that alley murder," he said, shouting and glowering at me from where he sat, across the table. He spoke in a rich baritone, the kind of voice you'd expect from a huge man with a look of world-weary cynicism. At six-foot-two and over 200 pounds, I was a big man and no weakling. But L.C. towered over me.

He sat back, bare-chested, his arms bulging "pythons," as a body builder would call them. He had the hard body of a man half his years. His chest was slabbed with thick muscles. His black skin glistened with a sheen of sweat, as did his clean-shaved head. A close trimmed full gray beard suited him – a symbol of wisdom. He'd arrived at his accompanying hard attitude honestly, from living in the brutal world of the black inner city.

"Earl Jones was beggin' to be killed," L.C. continued. "And

his girlfriend, Kim Artic, she was City Councilman Hayward Artic's daughter. And that fucked-up Four Dead tattoo tells me Reggie knows more. Hell, he was involved and thinks he's a big shot, in order to carve that insane name on his body. And he knows better than to piss me off."

I sat with my own rather modestly sized arms folded and resting on the tabletop, my chin propped on top of them.

"And as far as a 'auntie' go – shit, Roniece got no goddamn auntie," he said.

Hearing about Councilman Artic's daughter had been surprising, but nothing else was. At best, I'd dug a shallow ditch during my interview with Four Dead, and I still had no real interest in the case. I began glancing around the room, and couldn't help noticing that L.C.'s kitchen was utterly without furnishings. No curtains or shades on the old-fashioned high windows. The walls were freshly painted white, but were completely bare. The refrigerator was pulled away from the wall. A broom leaned against the wall next to the refrigerator. Dirty dishes in the sink.

"You hear a *goddamn* word I said?" L.C. asked, lowering his voice but emphasizing each word through gritted teeth.

I snapped my head away from looking at the sink and stared at him. My wide eyes and shocked expression were completely exaggerated.

He knew my sarcasm, and that I wasn't really offended, but he apologized anyway. "Sorry, bro'. My nerves are spikin'." He reached his hand across the table and I reached over to pat it gently, one time.

I withdrew my hand from his. "I agree with you about Four Dead's tattoo. Of course, he denied any connection with the murders, but he had a cat-that-ate-the-canary grin when he said it."

L.C. had grown remarkably calm in a short while. He crossed his hands on the table in front of him, adopting the pose of a preacher. In fact, he was reverent, and always struggled to be a man of peace, and a man of God. He had gotten better at it than anyone could have dreamed, from his heyday as a "troubled youth."

"And Four Dead can play one of the ultimate legal cards – he's certifiably crazy," I said.

L.C. leaned back, brought his hands up, and folded his arms

over his chest. He squinted at me. "What do you mean?"

"Did you know he's a schizophrenic? He seems under some control now, but I'll bet that's where all the wild vision stuff and his tattoo came from, before they got him on meds."

"You mean, he's insane?"

"It would take hard-assed testing to prove legal insanity, but being schizo makes his word really tough to sell in the legal arena." I looked around the kitchen again, and pointed at L.C.'s bare windows. "I'd be happy to help you with decorating."

He waved his hand at me. "You're always playin', Blanchard."

I looked back at him with dead seriousness. "I'm not playing, L.C. I'm gonna be brutal. Unless we get more than this hairball Four Dead has given us to work with, you'd be getting more from me if I'd help you decorate your kitchen windows." That door-slamming, I-want-off-this-job feeling clunked around inside me again. I leaned toward him and said, "There's a lovely window treatment on sale at Target right now." I'd lowered my voice to an unnatural decibel level when I spoke.

The look in his eyes told me got it. That was the thing about our relationship – we could talk plainly to each other.

I placed my hands on the table and interlaced my fingers. "We got nothing but worthless speculation, right now, L.C. And, anyway – we're trying to find your missing sister, not solve any homicides."

He sighed heavily and brought one hand to his throat. I stared at the table, thinking. The murder of Hayward Artic's daughter had been big news when it happened, but I hadn't made the connection while talking to what Four Dead said. Four Dead had to have known she was the councilman's daughter, and failing to mention it was a strike against him. But then, being a mental patient was already *three* strikes against him.

I shifted in my chair and cleared my throat. "I remember hearing about that Jones murder, now. Do you think Roniece had been involved with Jones?"

"I'd heard she and Reggie were dealing for Jones, but I don't know for sure."

"Even if she had been, it's farfetched that she'd be on the run today because of a two-year-old murder."

"She's been in the dope world a long time. She could know lots of people who want to make her disappear."

We looked each other in the eye.

"Yeah, I think she could be dead," he said, in a steely tone. "Killed by the dope wars and tossed in some dumpster. Who the hell knows?"

The sun had been streaming heat and light through the windows behind me. I'd left my jacket on, an old habit, even when I was warm. I'd mentioned that once to a police department shrink who told me I had a deep-seated need to flee at a moment's notice. I told him I was sorry I mentioned it.

I took off my jacket. My T-shirt had sweat stains flowing from my armpits to my waist.

At length, L.C. sighed and slumped a little. The glare he'd had the entire time I'd been there had left his eyes. The deep furrows running the width of his brow remained – they were permanently etched into his flesh.

"Well, think of what he told me that you hadn't known about," I said.

"There ain't much. Just the auntie bullshit. There's nothin' new about Earl Jones and Kim Artic, and I ain't convinced it's got anything to do with Roniece bein' missing. But Roniece and me are from different generations. I don't have ins with her homeys. No one would tell me shit – not that I bothered asking. No doubt a rival dealer killed Jones and the others. But Roniece? Involved with all that drama? Who knows what's true?

"And this so-called auntie must be someone who lets her stay at her place. If there even is anyone."

"That's what you have me for," I said. "If the auntie exists, I'll find her. What about that bar on J Street?"

"Aquarius? I know the place, been there twice since Roniece disappeared. The cops went there, too, after I reported her missing. Everyone claimed they don't know her."

This time my shocked look was real. "Whoa, L.C., what the hell else haven't you told me?"

"It was already done. I thought you wanted new stuff."

"You thought wrong. I gotta know everything, check everything myself."

L.C.'s habits from the paranoid circles in which he'd once traveled were hard to break – he played his cards close. But this was too important.

"All right," I said. "Before we say another word, is there anything else?" I was annoyed, and he knew it.

"Sorry," he said meekly. "But there's nothing else."

L.C.'s reticence alerted me. I didn't trust him not to know more, despite his assurance that there wasn't more. And Four Dead – his mental problems would overwhelm his self-control. When this happened he'd be likely to do anything: hold back, tell the truth dead on, or make up stories. Probably a mixture of all three, which would be worst of all. His schizophrenia pulled the levers and pushed the buttons in his brain, but his fear of L.C. sometimes popped through and stopped him cold. But it was all too hazy. We'd just have to work with what he'd said.

I decided to be play a hard card. "I'll bet anything *someone* who hangs at Aquarius knows Roniece. And I'll bet this so-called auntie is a real person."

He arched his brow, a hope-against-hope look in his eyes. "You think you got something to work with?"

L.C. needed to hear something hopeful. I was his buddy, not just a PI he'd hired. Besides, when I found nothing, or found the worst, he wouldn't blame me. He knew whose fault it would be.

I shrugged and raised my hands, palms up. "Well, it's something for me to look into."

L.C. reached across the table, grabbed my arm and pulled it toward him. His eyes had softened, sprouting moisture.

"You once worked a miracle for me," he said, letting my arm go. "Now my baby sister needs one. And more than just being found – she needs to turn her life around."

"There's a chance you'll know more about her going missing than you did before."

He brought a hand up to his eyes and squeezed away the tears threatening to expose his soft heart. The look in his eyes had generally mellowed since the first time I saw them years earlier, when they peered out from the face of a sad and angry man sitting across from me in Waupun – the same way Four Dead had sat across from me earlier this day. L.C. had eventually – and quite ironically – become the best friend I'd ever had.

"So, what do you think, Chief?" he asked, after refolding his hands on the table, resuming his pastor-like demeanor. He frequently called me that, both with affection and playful mockery. His tone this time couldn't have been more serious.

I had no choice but to remain upbeat. I readjusted myself in my chair and smiled at him. "I'll hit the beach a-runnin'. I'll go to Aquarius and talk to people." I had little confidence that I'd get anywhere, but L.C. was going to get my best effort.

"I'll come with you," L.C. said.

I could feel my smile shrink, ever so slightly. "I never take clients with me. And you already swung twice and missed."

"Yeah, but this is different. And I think I can stir more up than you, if you know what I mean." He rubbed his face, kept his palms toward himself and held his arms out toward me.

I rubbed my own face and stretched my hands out before me. "Yeah, the color thing. Anyway, how well do you actually know the place?"

"I don't hang around there. Too many crack asses."

"How did they act toward you?"

He looked thoughtful. "All right. Some people knew my rep. They got polite real quick." His expression suddenly grew stony. "My good rep, not the bad. People know my story, and my business spreads my name."

He'd become a building contractor, focusing on rehabbing inner city homes. He was the most honest, hardest working operator in the business, and people revered him for it I knew he was well regarded, but I hadn't known respect for him extended to the "crack asses." No wonder he still had influence with the prison inmates.

After a long moment, I said, "But no one there knew Roniece? I don't believe that. The cops coming around and asking questions held them back, I'm sure."

"That's what I figured. But I didn't think it was time to throw my weight around. I wanted to soft pedal it, so I called you."

"So, you think I'm soft, huh? What happened to calling me

'Chief'?"

He made a weak smile that told me he wasn't able to joke.

"Sorry. I'm trying to help you, too."

He reached over and touched my arm again. "I know you are, brother. I thought I hated that little bitch." He looked at me hard. "Yeah, I mean bitch. She hurt our family. She's the only one off track. My two full sisters are married with kids – one's married to a cop – and I cleaned up a long time ago. I get so mad, so damn mad. . . ."

Tears brimmed and slipped down his face. The last of his toughness and pride spilled out with them. His chin quivered for a moment. He quickly regained control. He didn't bother to wipe his tears. I studied him. His sad, dark look overwhelmed his magnificent features – his large head and wide face, prominent cheekbones, his nose and lips in perfect proportion to the rest. Laugh lines sprawling away from his eyes had become gutters for the tears he cried. I hadn't known he'd cared about his sister that much. I hadn't seen him look that unhappy since the day years before when I met him at the prison.

"I never met Roniece," I said. "She must have her good ways." I'd never met his other family, either. He kept me away from some parts of his life.

"*Humph*. I ain't doin' this for her. She and I have the same father, and he's dead. He'd always asked me to watch out for her, even though he knew it was hopeless. And her mama, well, she's good people. Roniece's broken her heart."

"So, you and Roniece aren't on the best of terms?"

"No. I get emotional about the whole thing because I've just seen too much. Drugs fucked her up. She'd go clean for a while and come home to her mother's. Then she'd fuck up and go back to the street. But we could always send word around, and she'd call or send word back. Not this time."

"Where was she living when she – "

"Disappeared," he said, finishing my sentence for me. "That's the scary part. She'd been clean for a long stretch, livin' with her mama. Then one day last week she didn't come home. I can't stop thinkin' old business caught her."

"Maybe she just needed a break, and this was her way of taking one."

"Maybe she gave up and went back on the pipe. That's my best hope." It was a sad dilemma for a man – hoping his sister was only smoking crack cocaine, and not dead.

We agreed to get something to eat, and then go together to Aquarius.

CHAPTER FOUR

In the early evening we went to the Aquarius tavern on J Street. L.C. had parked over a block away so we could sneak up on the tavern – crack asses would run if they saw him coming, he'd explained, and they'd be our best witnesses. Rapidly growing dusk was settling upon us. We walked on an ancient, crumbling sidewalk with thick grass growing between each slab. Spidery fissures lined the cement in all directions. Large chunks of concrete were missing everywhere.

Long rows of vacant lots, every one once occupied by a small business or house or apartment building, loomed ahead on both sides of the street. The street was dark and desolate, a victim of inner city blight. The tavern was at the foot of a steep hill. I was grateful L.C. was with me.

"Just so you know, I'm packing," I said, just before we entered the tavern.

"Got it covered myself." He patted his waist.

We'd be as protected as we could be in a bar full of criminals, all packing guns that were aching to feel an itchy trigger finger.

The tavern was smaller than I'd imagined – not much bigger than a large living room. It was early – 8:30 p.m. – and the bar was full. Everyone there was African American. I could almost hear the mumbled conversations retreating to the back room while our entry silenced the place. No music was playing. Cigarette smoke hung thickly in the air, despite new laws against such activity. Everyone stared at L.C., a six-foot, six-inch black man who looked as though he could twist someone's head off. He'd dressed humbly, wearing a plain, dark blue shell jacket and loosely fitting khaki slacks. I looked ridiculously out of place in my Harley jacket, T-shirt, and jeans – never mind my skin color. But all eyes were on him. I felt safe. L.C. was indeed a scary guy.

He looked around. I stayed close to him, like his second skin.

He stopped and looked around the bar. "Some of them saw me in here before," he said while turning back to me. "The whole place will know about it."

He turned and moved forward to one end of the bar and motioned the bartender toward him. I followed like a dazed puppy.

L.C. pointed to me. "This is Jack Blanchard, a friend of mine," he said in a low voice to the bartender, a small and frail black man in his 40s with nervous eyes and a twitching face. He clearly did not like seeing us in his place.

L.C. continued. "He's checkin' some shit out for me." He reached back and placed his hard, heavy arm across my shoulders.

I smiled and offered the man my hand. He weakly reached toward it and gave it a dead-fish handshake. His hand was cool and damp. He quickly withdrew it.

L.C. stepped back and looked around the bar again. I paused and looked, also. The lack of music was eerie. The scent of marijuana hung heavily, along with the slowly sinking blue cloud of cigarette smoke. Bottles and glasses clinked. A few people drank their drinks. A few snickered. A leather-clad man and woman wearing shades mumbled to each other.

I motioned the bartender close and he leaned toward me.

"I'm an investigator," I said, "and I'm trying to find my friend's missing sister, Roniece Veasley. Word is she hangs around here, but so far everyone here has said they don't know her." I pointed my thumb over my shoulder at L.C. while still looking at the bartender. "My friend doesn't believe it. You know who he is?"

The bartender nodded. "L.C. Veasley. He know me, too, from community business meetings." He spoke in a soft, dry voice.

"You own this place, then?"

"Yeah."

"Good. I think we can get somewhere. I'm convinced Roniece

hangs around here, too."

"Uh-huh. But not for a while."

L.C. glowered at the small man, who seemed to grow even smaller. I was suspicious. It was too easy. Why would the owner tell me – a white PI – and not L.C. – an iconic African American known throughout the city – when he'd come in before?

"I'm tired of the heat," he said, as though he'd read my mind. "L.C. and the cops comin' in all the time bad for 'bidness. She ain't been here for a long time. Couple months, I'd guess."

He made sense but I was distrustful by nature, a result of my past experiences. I can't get rid of my distrust of people. It hangs on the way chewed bubble gum from a sidewalk sticks to your shoe.

"Does anyone in here know her?" I asked, looking back and raising my voice.

He put his head down and quickly stepped away. He served some drinks and appeared to be finished talking to me. Two customers left. He said good-bye to them. He looked at me with hard eyes. I motioned for him to return to me. He moved reluctantly, stopping to ask each customer on the way if they needed another drink.

"I think more of your business is gonna take a hike," I said to him in a low voice when he finally reached me. "I mean, if L.C. and me left, that probably wouldn't happen."

"Give me your card," he said in a barely audible whisper.

More people in the crowd began talking among themselves. A few more looked as though they were ready to leave.

I slipped him a business card. He shoved it into his pocket without looking at it.

"See if anyone knows of an auntie where she goes to crash," I said.

He turned and walked away again. I looked behind me and L.C. wasn't there, having turned to walk among the crowd. People were moving away from him as though he were a coming plague. In his place next to me were several stern dark faces with unfriendly eyes. They'd crowded me in, giving the clear message they weren't about to move. I looked over their heads and called out, "L.C.," in a business-like, steady voice. It was a good act. Good for me, that was. I was sure my new acquaintances weren't the least impressed.

L.C. bulldozed his way toward me, parting the group with an effortless brush of his arms. They moved easily, a couple of them giggling. "Just jivin'," they seemed to say. L.C. gave me an inquiring look, and I nodded. He turned and walked toward the door and I quickly followed. The crowd parted once again for him and stayed spread for me while I walked past. Everyone grew silent once again while we left.

We walked back up the hill toward L.C.'s car. L.C. strode head down, hands jammed into his pockets, ramming against the night. I jogged trying to keep up with him.

"Well, what do you think?" I asked.

The separation between us was growing. I had to yell.

"I think it's a dead end," he called back to me.

"Why?"

He continued pushing the pace.

I stopped and shouted, "L.C., slow up. We gotta talk."

He stopped and turned toward me, a disgusted look on his face. "Nothin' to talk about."

"Wait a minute. Tell me what you're thinking."

We stood beneath a street lamp, which lit the devastated landscape, L.C., and me.

"Elmore ain't gonna call you," L.C. said.

"Who?"

"Elmore Harris, the bar owner. He took your card to stall. He said a little something about Roniece to keep it cool. But he ain't gonna call."

"I wasn't going to hold my breath, but what happened in there is better than nothing. I've worked in tighter places than this and eventually got what I wanted." That wasn't really true, but it was part of my pitch.

"I'm gonna have to take another route," L.C. said, more to himself than to me. He sounded both resigned and determined. "I gotta create some real pressure, after all." He took a step backward and started to turn.

"Wait," I said. "Wait, wait, wait." I stepped toward him. "Let's give it a day, just to keep our thoughts straight. We're both tired. Let's both go home and sleep on it, and I'll call you tomorrow morning."

He hesitated a brief moment. "Call my cell phone. I'll be out and about."

He was just feeling tempted – he still wanted to do things the right way. I looked up at him. He stood several paces above me on the hill, towering over me to a frightening degree. His head seemed to scrape the black sky.

We quietly stared at each other. Then he said, "I've got some properties to check tomorrow, some work to do. I'll wait a day before I make a move."

"Good. Thanks. We don't want to do anything rash. There's still things that can be done."

"Like what?"

"You leave that to me, okay?"

He sighed. "Okay, I'll leave that to you."

We walked more slowly toward his car, got in, and drove in silence back to his house. I could only imagine what he was thinking. I was thinking one thought, over and over – what the hell was I going to do now?

CHAPTER FIVE

Sleep couldn't find me that night. Images of L.C. roiled in my mind, making knots in my stomach. His soul suffering over Roniece had gotten to me in ways I hadn't felt since I'd worked on his case when he was in prison. My lack of confidence that I could find her made even bigger knots. I eventually slept fitfully, the bedclothes dampened with sweat and squeezing around me like a coiling snake.

I got up at my usual time – 6:30 a.m. – put on coffee and toasted a bagel, and sat at the kitchen table, shirtless and in my light blue pajama bottoms, while waiting for the coffee and bagel to finish. I felt all right, in spite of my bad night. I turned on the computer but decided not to pick anything over until later. Bar owner Elmore Harris would be my number one.

The morning newspaper contained its usual drivel, but I sat at the table and read it anyway. It was another warm, sunny day, and I put on my shorts, tank top, and Reeboks after I finished my bagel and cup of coffee. Walking through my neighborhood, feeling the breeze tease my leg hairs, petting a couple dogs and ignoring their owners at the other end of the leash, made me feel better.

Afterward, I showered and, wrapped in my bathrobe, sat in my favorite lounge chair in the living room and channel-hopped the network and cable news shows on TV. Electronic drivel. I finally turned to a local station. An attractive woman talk-show hostess with short, dark hair and wearing a sensible, blue business suit sat on a sofa, interviewing a young local writer who'd gotten her first novel published. The hostess stopped and looked away from her guest and past the camera toward someone who'd obviously signaled to her. She then said, "We are now switching to some breaking news."

The scene switched to a conference room in City Hall, with the mayor and top police officials standing together in front of a microphone and podium. Behind them hung an oversized city flag. Reporters, obviously summoned to the room in haste, rushed pell-mell to their seats.

Mayor Arthur McCord, a handsome and popular mayor, strode to the podium, and everyone grew quiet. He was dressed impeccably as always, in a blue-gray suit, matching tie, and white shirt. His medium-brown hair was combed perfectly, but the look of deep agony marred his face. For a moment I thought he might cry.

"I have tragic news to announce," he said with a slight tremolo in his voice. "Early this morning, Marilyn Chase, my Chief of Staff, was found dead in Lincoln Park. Her body has been positively identified. Her loss is a severe one to our community, as she was a longtime, dedicated public servant. She was also one of my most competent and trusted aides. She will be deeply missed."

"She was your girlfriend," I said out loud. It was the worst kept secret in town.

The mayor continued. "I'm not at liberty to discuss any details of her death, nor will I take any questions. Chief Rhodes of the police department will answer whatever questions he is able."

The mayor stepped away from the podium, and Chief Jerome Rhodes moved to it. "Dusty Rhodes," we used to call him when I was on the force – an absurd nickname, which had been the point. He was the epitome of a military-sharp dresser, and an organized, hard-working detective. One of the best I'd ever known. And I knew him well – he was my partner for two years on the Homicide Squad before he was promoted to Lieutenant of Detectives.

The chief wore full uniform dress and answered polite questions from the shocked reporters, most of whom probably knew Marilyn Chase well. The chief answered in vague terms. I wondered why the hell he answered any questions at all – what little the police knew would be kept confidential anyway. Listening to Dusty speak, I remembered why the mayor had him do so many press conferences.

He was smooth and assuring and had a way of making you think he'd told you a lot, when he'd told you next to nothing. He had a future in politics.

He did say the matter was being treated as a homicide, but the police had no leads. He wasn't ready to divulge the manner of death. Also, the public would be notified of whatever details he could supply without compromising the investigation. It was all hot air, but people had to hear something.

Other top police brass stood near him at the podium. Prince White, Chief of Detectives, stood immediately to Chief Rhodes's left. Assistant Chief Mary Calavito stood next to White. Two other top commanders, a man and a woman, both wearing uniforms and the obligatory ton of brass, stood next to Assistant Chief Calavito.

The press conference ended. A burly, dark haired man with a thick mustache, wearing a dark business suit, approached Mayor McCord on his right, and touched his shoulder. The mayor seemed on the verge of collapse. The man held his arm while they walked from podium. A male reporter describing the scene identified the man in the suit as Detective Vincent Dragos of the police department, the mayor's personal aide and driver.

I'd never seen the young detective before. He probably hadn't even been on the force when I left. I felt old. But then, so what? I *was* old.

Marilyn Chase had been an excellent government employee. Smart and honest, she'd burned the midnight oil and had a legendary sense of humor. She was drop-dead beautiful, with long, natural golden-blond hair, a movie star's face, and a perfect figure.

I had a wife once who actually looked similar, but....

The word was that Marilyn had been every bit as sweet and charming as she looked. But she could pour on the hard-as-nails routine in an angry instant and had brass balls as big as those in the bells of the Notre Dame Cathedral. In a sweet, charming sort of way. She was at times a jut-jawed fury who'd gladly go on TV and verbally carve up an upstart Common Council member who tried pulling fast ones on his or her constituents, or in City Hall. On such occasions she'd spoken softly, in an almost mockingly patient tone, but got her point across with articulate and deadly accuracy.

Of course, she carried a big stick – the full effect of the mayor's political power. Some had found it necessary to mention that he provided her with another stick, but that was the kind of sordid talk I'd never listened to, nor passed along.

I turned off the TV. Huh. Murder at City Hall. The dead body of the mayor's lover in a park near the lakefront. I'd have loved to be investigating it. The mayor, of course, would be my suspect. He and Marilyn were both single but decided to keep their relationship out of the spotlight, which took away the married-man-with-a-mistress-on-the-side motive and subplots thereof. But without any other leads, he would still be my – and every cop's – number one suspect.

It was 9:30, and I'd drunk three more cups of coffee, which meant I couldn't wander too far from a toilet. Staying home would have to do. Waiting for something to happen with Roniece Veasley's case, like waiting for time to stop, would likely take up my whole day. I did want to call L.C. to see how he was doing – if he were keeping his promise not to go nuclear. For that, I'd also wait.

I hadn't yet checked any records on the case. I always waited until just before I started the job for that. What if paperwork got entered on someone between the time I checked and the time I left? It was one of my obsessive quirks, and it didn't bother me, so didn't take pills to help me stop it. After quickly finishing the newspaper crossword puzzle while sitting once again at my kitchen table, my phone rang.

I answered it. "Jack Blanchard Investigations."

"You for real?" a determined sounding woman with a husky voice said.

"Excuse me?"

"I want to know if you for real."

"Of course, I'm for real. Who's calling?"

"You not the police? You a private eye?"

"Private as they come. How can I help you?"

"Maybe I'll talk to you later," the woman said, and hung up.

Damn it. It had to have been Roniece. I should have hit her up right away, and not tried schmoozing her. I used the dial-back function on my phone, and after one quick ring a recorded woman's voice said the number had "dialing out" capabilities only. A public telephone. Who the hell used them anymore? People who forgot their cell phones, and dope dealers. And other people who don't want to be traced, for whatever reason. Roniece fit all three possibilities.

I'd been caught off guard, and I was angry with myself. L.C. wouldn't be happy, but I had to tell him I thought Roniece had called.

I tried L.C.'s home and cell phone numbers and had to leave messages on both. Rising stomach acid burned in me like molten lava. My caffeine buzz turned to pure anxiety. I'd peed twice in the past half hour, and another was coming on strong. Pinned down in my house, waiting to pee some more and steeling myself against L.C.'s anger when he called back and I told him what had happened, I felt like a rat slowly sinking into a meat grinder.

An hour went by and L.C. hadn't called. I mindlessly channel-hopped on the TV. I stood up and walked to the underground garage of my apartment building, got in my car, and began driving around aimlessly, which made me more anxious. I should have figured as much. Lunch at my favorite deli didn't help. Peeing again at a gas station helped for as long as the relief lasted. Back to driving aimlessly, I heard my cell phone ring.

"Jack Blanchard Investigations," I said, my heart in my throat. I pulled to the curb on a side street.

"Somethin's come up."

It was L.C.

"What?" I asked, trying not to shout. "What is it?"

"Come to my place, right away. I'll explain when you get here." He hung up before I could respond.

I drove recklessly toward his house, like someone who'd drunk too much coffee.

Once inside, L.C. mumbled a perfunctory greeting and directed me to sit on the same kitchen chair as the day before. Sunlight filled the room, but was not yet on my back. L.C. again sat across the table from me.

"Did you get a call this morning?" he asked. His voice was calm, almost silky.

"Yeah, from a woman asking if I was really a private dick, or a cop. She hung up after that. I think it was Roniece."

"It wasn't."

"Well, then who? . . . How do you know?"

"The woman called me, too. I'm in the phone book because of my business. Wouldn't give me her name. She said she'd been at Aquarius yesterday. She said she'd sat close enough to overhear your conversation with Elmore. Said she'd heard your name and looked up your number, too."

I tried remembering any women sitting that close. The place had been too crowded, with too many faces to absorb and remember. Not that I'd bothered trying. I drew a blank.

L.C. continued. "She knows Roniece, and she'd heard about the times me and the cops came in. She's worried if Roniece's all right."

"Does she know how to contact her?"

"She told me where she's staying."

"With her auntie?"

"I told you she's got no auntie. The woman said she's been in touch with her."

"Roniece?"

"Right. She stayed at a dope house for a night, then on the street for a night 'cause she supposedly don't do dope no more. I don't believe it, but it don't matter right now."

"Where is she now?"

He paused and drew a breath. He looked at me with one skeptical eyebrow cocked, and said, "Get this. She's supposed to be in a women's shelter. Believe that? A women's shelter?"

"Those are for battered women. Does she have a boyfriend?"

"I don't know."

"Somebody had to knock her around. They send the homeless to the Rescue Mission."

"Nothing would surprise me."

"Well, at least we have something solid to check."

"Not so fast," L.C. said. "She may not be there anymore, and anyway, those shelters don't tell *anybody* if someone's there."

"I know. But we'll go and show our IDs. Those places cooperate a little. If she's there, they'll deliver a message to her if they think we're okay."

"Really? I thought they'd hide her."

"They will if that is what she wants. Then you won't get through to her. But we've got nothin' to lose."

We got in my car and drove the mile or so from L.C.'s house to the Pathfinders Women's Shelter. At the counter inside we met a polite, young white woman wearing no make-up and silver-colored, wire-rimmed glasses, with dark hair woven into a thick braid that reached her waist. She looked at L.C.'s identification.

"Please leave your name and phone number," she said dryly. "We'll check to see if anyone here wishes to call you."

I placed my business card on the counter in front of her. L.C. reached in his wallet for a card and also placed it on the counter. She took them both.

"She's been reported missing to the police," L.C. said. "That must mean something to you."

"Yes. The matter is between her and the police. If she's here, they'll cancel their missing report. But she still doesn't have to call you."

"Sounds like you've been through this before."

She made a slight, mirthless smile. "Every day."

We left and went back to L.C.'s house, and again sat in our respective chairs in the kitchen. L.C. was happy. Roniece was alive. I was happy. I didn't have to chase a wild goose.

"How about a beer?" L.C. asked, reaching for the handle of the refrigerator that was still pulled away from the wall and standing askew in the room.

"Let's see. My last drink was a week ago." I handed L.C. my cell phone. "Would you call my doctor and see if it's okay?"

He laughed curtly. "Bust my chops, my man, all you want." He fished two beers out of the refrigerator and turned to me. He held up the bottles and arched his brow. "I'll drink *both* of these."

"You got me, L.C. Gimme a beer." I reached out and he stuck a frosty bottle in my hand. I twisted off the top and took a deep swallow. The ice-cold beer went down sweetly. "If Roniece calls, or the police cancel their missing report, my work is done, my friend," I said after putting the bottle down and wiping my mouth. "It's up to her to tell the police about any problems she might have."

L.C. sat down after pulling a swig from his beer. "Yeah, but I want to get her back under my wing. I want our family to take care of her, give her what she needs. Especially for her mother's sake."

"I hope everything works out."

After a long moment, L.C. suddenly said, "I'm gonna call the cops, just for the hell of it." He got up and in flash was in his the living room calling the police.

I waited serenely, sucked my beer, smiled and prepared to daydream about the first nonsensical thing that popped into my mind.

L.C. stomped back into the kitchen. "I have to call back later to see if there's a change in Roniece's missing status," he said with exaggerated articulation, apparently mocking a too-serious police employee. He stood at his chair and chugged his beer, went to the refrigerator for another, and set another one before me also, even though I wasn't half finished with my first. We drank a couple more beers after that while talking casually.

L.C. dragged the chair loudly away from the table and sat down. "I can't take shit like this no more. I can't trust nobody no more." The affects of the beer couldn't stave off his rapidly darkening mood.

I brought my bottle from my lips and set it on the table. "I understand. You can't control your family's behavior. At least you can choose your friends."

"Shit, I don't have no friends. I don't *like* nobody."

"Does anyone like you?"

He ignored my tease and sipped his beer while staring off. "Don't know, don't care."

"I like you, L.C."

He looked askance at me, waved his hand, and turned his head.

"I don't just like you, I love you."

He looked at me again, a look of disgust crinkling his face.

"Did I ever tell you what a good looking man you are?"

His eyes widened, his jaw dropped. Then his is expression relaxed, and he smiled. "Something's wrong with you, Blanchard. Way wrong." He chuckled and looked away.

I laughed lightly with him.

He looked back at me, still smiling, eyes twinkling. "I love you, too, man. I just don't trust you. Want another beer?"

We continued laughing – silly, alcohol-fueled chuckles. I drank another beer.

I drove home slowly – too slowly, the way a drunk drives. A beery aura surrounded me, permeating my car's interior. I managed to park the car in the underground stall of my apartment, push and stagger through the closed door into the hallway, and stink up the elevator while riding up to my place. It was still light out, too light to be feeling drunker than an alley full of winos, the way I did. I plopped onto my living room lounge chair and tried watching TV with one eye open, but started to pass out. I got up, peeled off my clothes while walking to my bedroom, and crawled buck-naked into bed. This time, sleep had no trouble finding me and it pitched me down a bottomless black pit.

CHAPTER SIX

I'd slept for nearly eleven hours. It was light out again, but still early morning. The room smelled as though a drunk had been sleeping in it. Rolling to my side, I saw the blinking light of my telephone answering machine on the nightstand next to my bed. My cell phone stays in the kitchen when I go to bed. It rings alone, with no one to hear or care. When I'm sleeping, I'm sleeping.

I yawned and rubbed the sleep from my eyes. I didn't feel too bad. Apparently, I'd out-slept most of my hangover. I reached for the playback button on the answering machine.

"Jack, it's L.C. It's after four in the morning. I called the police around midnight and they'd cleared Roniece's case. And guess what? Roniece called me an hour ago from the shelter, and I went to get her. Call me when you hear this."

I was surprised and happy for him. I'd never felt better about having a case closed so quickly and successfully. I got up and went to the bathroom, noticing while passing through the living room that I'd left the TV on after going to bed. After splashing water from the bathroom sink onto my face and key body parts and rinsing my mouth three times, I went to the kitchen, grabbed the phone, and dialed L.C.'s number.

"How's everything?" I asked after he answered.

"She's here, but there's problems. I'd like you to talk to her."

"What about?"

"Some about what Reggie Thackery said, some about her. Can

you come over?"

"Sure. I'll be there as soon as I can."

After a mad dash to my car, I sped to L.C.'s house and soon sat with him and Roniece – me in an overstuffed chair against one wall, the two of them on a plush, black velvet couch in front of the picture window. Roniece had cleaned up her crack act pretty well – she looked healthy, but also distressed. Her clothes, a white sleeveless blouse and red Capri pants, were clean. There were no bruises or other marks on her face. She was pretty, with a round face and round eyes and short black hair, and resembled L.C. She squirmed in her seat and looked as though she didn't want to be there.

After introducing Roniece and me, L.C. turned to her and said, "Tell him what you told me."

"You tell him," she said curtly. "You know as much as I do." Her voice was scratchy, her tone defiant. A toxic mixture of hate and fear seemed to emanate from her. She adjusted herself, slouching in her seat. She seemed about to bolt for the door. I wondered why she'd left the shelter.

I leaned forward slightly, adopting and inquisitor's pose. "Are you scared?" I asked her.

She snorted and stared at the floor.

I looked at L.C.

"She's scared shitless," he said, leaning into one corner of the couch, folding his hands across his chest. "The dope world won't go away."

I nodded. "Why did they let you stay at the shelter?" I asked Roniece. "Someone beat you up?"

"No. Nobody beat me up." She wouldn't look at me.

"Then why did they let you stay there?"

"I know people." She grew more dismissive with each word. Her eyes bugged out slightly. She was going to offer no information whatsoever.

It was going to be tougher than talking to Four Dead, but I continued trying, out of respect for L.C. After ten minutes of me cajoling and her sidestepping, she finally admitted that she'd heard of Earl Jones, and knew about his murder two years earlier. She scoffed at what Four Dead told me, that she was in danger of being killed, saying he was crazy. And she denied being close friends with Kim Artic. "I knew who she was. Everyone know 'bout her. Her father's a councilman."

I didn't believe her denial.

"But I don't know nothin' 'bout Earl Jones's dope dealin,'" she said, in possibly the most unconvincing lie of any liar I'd ever heard. "Or nothin' about his murder." She sat still while talking, with only her jaw moving. She had perfect fuck-you body language.

I mentioned Reggie's "4 Dead" tattoo. "What do you think? Does it have something to do with Earl Jones' murder?"

She looked at me, rolled her eyes and shook her head. "He hear about it, like everybody in the street. In his crazy, motherfuckin' dreams, he involved. Reggie, he's nothin'. Never be nothin' but a crazy-ass jailbird."

L.C. and I looked at each other. He rolled his eyes. A disgusted look crossed his face.

"Call himself 'Four Dead,'" she said, muttering to herself. "Put a crazy-ass tattoo on his arm. He a schizo – a freak."

She grew silent. Her mouth curled up at the corners, furrows appeared on her brow. Fear was pushing anger off her face. Tension hung in the air.

"Why did you make yourself disappear?" I finally asked her.

She looked at L.C., then back at me. "Personal reasons." She wouldn't explain further. "I ain't talkin' 'bout it no more. It my goddamn business, and I'll take care of myself."

"Roniece, you're obviously scared, running to women's shelters for protection. How long can you take care of yourself that way?"

She neither looked at me nor responded.

"Why did you come back to L.C.'s, instead of your mother's?"

"I came here 'cause I was gettin' freaked at the shelter and it was too late at night to go home." She continued to look frightened, but apparently not yet afraid enough to tell the whole story. I wondered if she ever would be.

"You couldn't wait until morning and go to your mother's?" I asked.

She wouldn't answer. I was done begging for answers, and

stood to leave. "I'm glad you're safe, Roniece. Maybe you and L.C. can work this out."

A helpless look crossed L.C.'s face, while Roniece's expression grew vacant. She sat with her elbow on her knee and her chin resting on her upraised fist. She gently rocked forward and back.

I shook L.C.'s hand, which felt cool and spongy. We said goodbye, and I left L.C.'s house. The case was solved, I thought after getting to my car and heading home. Great. Not great. Roniece was obviously running from someone – probably involving an old drug deal – and only she could make it stop. I wondered why she wouldn't call the police. That would be her best chance, if she were really out of the drug scene. I agreed with Four Dead and L.C. – she likely had trouble that could make her dead. The kind of trouble the authorities couldn't help her with.

Once in my apartment, I made myself a pot of coffee and a ham and cheese sandwich. I sat in front of my computer at the kitchen table, but remembered that I had no need to use it. The last remnants of my hangover were gone. I had no work to do. All my other cases were pending, waiting for return phone calls and other correspondence. It was back to being idle, and that suited me just fine.

CHAPTER SEVEN

Two days later at around 10:00 a.m., I was sitting in my lounge chair drinking tepid coffee from my *Stinking Badge* cup and watching cable TV news. I was essentially ignoring my clients, and the telephone rang. The TV show was so inane, I immediately forgot what I had been watching when I answered the phone.

"Jack, it's me, L.C." He sounded serious.

I sat up, a sense of dread growing within me. I knew why he was calling.

"Roniece took off again," he said. "She was staying with me, and she took off. Yesterday morning."

"Why didn't you call me then?"

"I didn't want to. I still don't want to, but I need you again."

I felt a bit less sorry for him than I had before, when she'd disappeared without notice and he'd had good reason to fear she'd been killed.

"Did she give any hints as to why she left?" I asked.

"Shit. She didn't say one damn word to me the whole time she stayed here."

I sat back in the chair and use the remote to turn off the TV. "How did she act otherwise?"

"She stayed in her room a lot, never left the house."

I started feeling more sorry for him again. "L.C., Four Dead may have been more accurate than we thought. Roniece could well have been involved with Earl Jones, and is still running from some bad deal. I'll check Jones's murder out with the police. Whatever it is, she's scared. Scared to death."

"Me too, brother. Me too."

We discussed how to proceed. I'd contact the Open Records Bureau of the police department to see what I could read about the murder of Earl Jones and his three companions. There wouldn't be much available information – uncleared criminal investigations are almost exclusively confidential.

L.C. said he'd go back to Aquarius to speak with Elmore Harris in private. He'd try to find out who the woman was who called us after overhearing my conversation with Harris. That was the only way we could play it – we agreed I was unlikely ever to get anything from the bar myself.

"We've got to find someone who knows why she's running scared," I said. "I'll go back to the women's shelter and see if they'll help." Fat chance.

While getting dressed, I turned on the radio in the kitchen and caught the 11 a.m. news in progress:

"Mayor McCord and Marilyn Chase are reported to have had an ongoing personal relationship," the female reporter with a no-nonsense voice said. Obviously in the middle of the story, she continued. . . . "Rumors of their affair had been circulating for some time. A mayoral spokesperson stressed that both were divorced, and they kept their relationship quiet to avoid unwanted publicity. An unnamed source said Ms. Chase was about to leave her office at City Hall to join the Governor's staff in the state's capital city."

"Well, Artie boy, they've got you in their sights," I said aloud while combing my hair in the bathroom. "What about Marilyn leaving City Hall? Leaving you, too? A motive? It's all no surprise, even to you, I'm sure. A little late on announcing the 'secret,' though." It had been one of the longer out-loud thoughts I'd had recently, which meant I didn't have enough to do.

I went to my car in the underground garage and drove off toward the Pathfinders Women's Shelter, hoping I could talk someone into delivering a message to whomever might know something about Roniece. I had a sneaking hunch the anonymous woman who'd called L.C. and me knew more about Roniece's trials and tribulations. Maybe she was the one to whom I should send a message.

"Hi, again," I said while breezing through the front door of the women's shelter and approaching the counter. The same detached but polite woman with whom I'd spoken the other day got up from her desk and met me at the counter.

She smiled, the same exact smile she'd given L.C. and me the last time.

"I, ah, I guess you know why I'm here," I said. I drummed my fingers on the counter top and smiled my I-know-I'm-not-getting-anywhere smile. I'm never presumptuous with someone who has already tossed me out once.

She continued smiling. Her expression darkened a bit, and she had a look that told me no one hoses her and lives to talk about it.

Nevertheless, I lowered my head and stooped slightly – the opening move of my subservient dog routine. It's my instinct, no matter what. Women are suckers for it all the time.

Her gaze grew stony. Her body language hardened. Maybe she didn't like dogs.

"I'm trying to get information that goes beyond a women's shelter kind of thing," I said, dropping all pretense of charming her. I leaned with both elbows on the counter. "I'm simply asking if you can pass along a message. Like the other day."

"A message to whom?" she asked, her smile gone and most likely her patience, as well.

"Oh, maybe Roniece Veasley, if she's been around. Or anyone else who wants to call me. I'm thinking someone outside the shelter knows something that could be important to her family. If they somehow got my number, they might try to help. As I said, there could be more here than meets the eye."

"There's always more than meets the eye with guys like you." She smiled again, one of those sly, inscrutable smiles that could either mean, "You're okay," or "Go pound rocks up your ass."

I assumed the latter, since that's what those smiles usually meant when directed at me.

"Well, then, do we have a deal?" I asked.

"Same rules apply to everyone, including you."

"That means yes?"

"Yes."

"Great." I reached into my jacket pocket.

"I still have your card, if that's what you're looking for."

"Right. Thank you. Didn't mean to be an annoyance."

She kept her same grin. "Time will heal."

Ha! I *knew* she meant I should go pound rocks.

I understood her reluctance to deal with me – second time in the shelter, concerning the same woman. And I was a PI, which to the women's shelter was the same as a cop. The shelters are leery of cops and don't like men trying to weasel their way into finding the women who are sheltered there.

While turning to leave I watched her straighten and square her shoulders, and once again give me her softer, hello/good-bye smile. She was a tough customer. For that, I respected her.

Getting to see the Earl Jones homicide file would take longer. I went to the Open Records Bureau at police headquarters and ordered a copy. This time a young, white male police aide in a policeman's uniform but wearing no gun waited on me at the counter. He couldn't have been more polite or eager to help. I watched wistfully while he virtually ran from the counter to make a phone call in back.

"The file will be ready tomorrow," he said.

His voice had a barely reached pubescent squeak in it. He had short, blond hair and a bright, rosy face. Being a cop would soon make it all dark and maybe mean looking. I didn't want to think about it.

I also remembered to check out the owner of Aquarius, Elmore Harris. He hadn't been arrested for anything serious in more than twenty years.

I wondered how L.C. was doing with the nervous Mr. Harris. Or, what he was doing *to* Mr. Harris. He'd call me when he was done, so I drove from the police station to the lakefront and parked in the sandy, tree-lined parking lot abutting the shoreline. I watched the rippling blue waters topped with tiny whitecaps that glided toward the shore. The sun blazed in the clear, azure sky. I'd parked beneath a shade tree, let down my windows, and sat back. A gentle breeze blew through the car. My mind drifted. I relaxed. The sound of the rolling water made me sleepy. My head fell back.

My ringing cell phone jarred me awake. "Jesus Christ," I said, feeling rudely interrupted. I ripped the offending phone from my waistband and pushed the answer button. "What is it?"

"Is this Jack Blanchard?" a pleasant, professional-sounding, woman's voice meekly asked.

I didn't recognize her voice. I hadn't dealt with a female client in months. "Yes. Who's calling, please?"

The woman paused and breathed out heavily. I could feel tension rising in her.

"This is Juanita Velez. The Pathfinders Women's Shelter passed along a message to me, regarding Roniece Veasley."

Dumbfounded, I paused to gather my thoughts. If any woman were to call about Roniece, I'd have expected it to be the anonymous woman who'd been at Aquarius when L.C. and I were there. She'd been the only one I could imagine would call after I left my message at Pathfinders.

"Juanita Velez? I'm sorry, but I—"

"Don't know me. I know. Are you truly a private detective? I need verification, because I'd like to talk to you if you are."

I gave her my PI license and agency numbers to check out. She said she'd call right back, and we hung up. I felt dazed and excited. All I could do was wait, and watch while the lake water gently massaged the shoreline.

A few minutes later the phone rang.

"This is Juanita Velez again. When can I speak with you?"

"Name the time and place."

"In my office, room 404, at City Hall. Three o'clock this afternoon."

City Hall. Jesus. "What do you do, there?"

"I'm head of the Social Services Department."

I managed to coolly say, "I'll be there."

She hung up.

I disconnected and tossed the phone to the passenger seat as though it were a hot brick. For a moment I felt nothing. My efforts at thinking felt like ungreased gears grinding themselves to pieces. Slowly, I recovered from my surprise. How the hell did City Hall get involved with a missing druggie? I didn't recall a Juanita Velez from the mayor's administration. She certainly wasn't high profile.

Considering that City Hall official Marilyn Chase had been murdered and Juanita Velez wanted to talk with me about Roniece Veasley, it couldn't have been a coincidence.

Three o'clock couldn't come soon enough.

My watch showed 12:45 p.m. L.C. hadn't called yet, which concerned me, but I had other onions to peel. I'd continue waiting for his call.

Killing time had proved agonizing, but I finally found myself walking into the stately gray building that housed City Hall. Built in the early twentieth century, it was a model of Gothic European architecture, with enormous brick archways at the entrance of the building. Several small spires rimmed the roof. A tower in front had a clock on its face with a bell inside that rang hourly. The building had been called "a work of art" and declared a national historical site. To me, it looked like a spooky old church, the kind that had a small city of catacombs beneath.

I was 15 minutes early and waited in the lobby. An atrium extended six stories up. The usual plants and flowers of such places were not in attendance. All the offices were situated along the building's outer walls. There was no activity, which I'd always found to be normal.

I idly gazed at mammoth paintings lining the walls – which to me were laughably tasteless – and acted like an awestruck tourist. I felt as though I didn't belong, and imagined blue-blazered security thugs with squawking walkie-talkies dragging me outside and beating the hell out of me.

Two minutes before three o'clock, I rode an elevator to the fourth floor. Room 404 was to my right. I nervously walked toward the door and tapped lightly on the door's large, pebbled glass panel. For some reason I felt the need to be sneaky. Partly a habit from my job, partly because being inside big government buildings unnerved me.

The dark outline of a woman approached and the door opened. The door squeaked when it swung wide. The woman stood before me. She had dark, shoulder-length hair, and wore a navy blue business suit with a knee-length skirt and a white blouse. She paused for a moment. I could feel her scrutinizing me. I looked into her eyes – dark brown and almond shaped, beneath long, curled eyelashes. She stared back, her expression blank. During the frozen moment, I observed her Latina beauty – her high, full cheekbones, straight, small nose, and voluptuous lips. Her skin was a light golden brown.

In the same moment I noticed I was staring, she invited me in.

"I assume you're Mr. Blanchard?" she said, stepping back to allow my entry. She was trim, her figure extremely well proportioned. Her voice was soft and sweet, contrasting with the rest of her demeanor. She radiated confidence and efficiency. She walked to a desk behind her and motioned for me to sit in a chair in front of it. I sat.

"And you're Juanita Velez, I assume?" I said. I asked in spite of a large sign on her desk with her name engraved.

"Oh, yes," she said, leaning over to shake my hand. "I'm sorry. It's hard to concentrate, with what's been going on."

Of course. She'd been Marilyn Chase's colleague. "I understand. Were you and Marilyn Chase close?"

She instantly looked sad but maintained her composure.

"Yes," she said. "We were close. Quite close, actually. Personally, as well as professionally."

"I'm sorry for your loss."

"Thank you."

She sat in her chair, obviously distracted, but made a strong effort to speak to me. "I'm the one who put Roniece Veasley up at Pathfinders Women's Shelter."

I couldn't have been more shocked. Roniece had been telling the truth when she said she knew people. I nodded but didn't speak, waiting for Ms. Velez to set the pace of the conversation.

She dispensed with preliminaries or small talk. The old-fashioned, high, narrow windows behind her desk allowed sunshine to pour into the room. The light silhouetted her, which accentuated her dark mood. She'd really been hit hard by Marilyn's death.

"I've known Roniece for about three months," she said, speaking slowly at first. "She'd checked into a health clinic about six months ago to get off her crack cocaine habit. The facilitators at the clinic worked with her, but sensed something more in her than a need to quit using drugs." She paused, brought one hand up to her brow and stuck an elbow onto the desktop to prop herself. She looked drained, near exhaustion.

"Thank you for calling me," I said. "How did you get to know Roniece?" I paused. "By the way, she'd left the shelter and was staying with her brother, and took off again. She's still missing."

"Oh, no. She must be in just terrible trouble." She slowly shook her head, breathed deeply, and continued. "I met her at the Women's Outreach Center. She had been off drugs for a while, was doing volunteer work, and seemed sincere. The woman in charge of the center vouched for her. A few weeks ago, I got her a job on my staff. She seemed happy about it. She came to work every day and did a decent job."

I was once again dumfounded. Either L.C. knew none of this, or he'd been holding back more information. If it were the latter, I'd be beyond furious. "What did she do?"

"Clerical things, delivering files, other odds and ends."

"Her family apparently knew none of this." *That had better be the case.*

"I know. For some reason, she wanted to keep this job to herself. She said she'd told her mother she was working at a car wash."

"Do you have any idea why she's been running away?"

"Only a vague one. She was at a job rally last week at the city's Summerfest grounds with Marilyn Chase. Marilyn had taken her along as an aide. While at the grounds, Roniece suddenly left, and never came back. Marilyn hadn't known Roniece before that day, and at first, didn't know why she'd leave that way. Marilyn told me later she'd thought of something, and that she was looking into it. She never said exactly what.

"Roniece called me a couple days later, and I got her into the women's shelter. I did so with no questions asked, but I did tell her to call Marilyn and explain herself. Then Marilyn" – her voice caught – "then Marilyn died, and I never knew what was on her mind about Roniece. Roniece hadn't said anything about why she ran when she called and asked for my help, but I could tell she was really scared. She said she'd never called Marilyn."

After a brief pause, she added, "There's one other thing. Marilyn did say she suspected there were some things going on that, once found out, would rock City Hall with scandal. I had the feeling she believed the incident with Roniece was part of it. That's the only hunch I have, and I know it's a poor one."

"And then Marilyn died right after what happened with Roniece," I said. "That's a suspicious coincidence." My inkling had been right, after all.

She sat in silence, a dark expression and far-off stare befalling her again.

I tried cheering her up. "By the way, the only bad thing about a hunch is if you don't at least think it through. Anything can be checked out and eliminated. It's a necessary part of any investigation."

She gave me a double take glance, and then kept her eyes on me.

The ball needed to roll again. "Might you have any ideas where Roniece stays when she's on the lamb?"

"No, I don't. Roniece never talked about her personal life. She has a very troubled past, and I fear she may be returning to it."

Juanita impressed me as an extraordinary woman. She exuded intelligence and wisdom – she was attractive in every way. My stomach fluttered. My heartbeat increased.

Another thought occurred to me. "Roniece supposedly knew a woman who'd been murdered over drugs a couple years back, although she denied it. The woman's father is Councilman Artic."

"Yes, that was Kim Artic. It had been well known that she was living with a drug dealer, who, along with Kim and two others, were all killed. Her father was scandalized, heartbroken."

"I don't suppose Roniece ever mentioned this Kim Artic."

"No."

"That's another one for the 'who knows?' pile."

She looked me in the eyes and made a slight smile. "I'll be of any assistance I can. You can call me any time. Here's my card."

I put the card in my pants pocket. "Thanks. The police can't chase after an adult who keeps taking off. They'll follow any leads that come in, especially involving females or people with health problems, but to my knowledge they don't have anything on Roniece right now. They should know about her working here, though."

"I'll call them." She added, "You're working for Roniece's

family, I take it?"

"Her half-brother, L.C. Veasley. That's the one she was staying with. He and I have a long history of helping each other."

"You sound like good friends."

"Great friends, actually. We've been through a lot together."

"I'll call you direct if there's a need."

"Yes. Always. But there are some things the police have to handle."

She leaned back in her chair. "Of course. I know the difference."

I felt small in my chair, in her presence. When she looked at me I felt paralyzed in a way that was both pleasing and disconcerting. I wanted to impress her. I felt like a schoolboy who wanted to sneak an apple onto his teacher's desk.

She stood, my cue to leave. After standing I extended my hand to her. She shook it. Her hand was warm and soft.

"I'll be doing my level best, Juanita. This will be my only case until it's solved, so I'll always be available."

This will be my only case? Where the hell had that come from? I was trying to impress her, that's where it had come from.

I hadn't let her hand go. She hadn't pulled away. She smiled again, this time warmly. A shock wave went through me. I meekly smiled back and finally pulled my hand from hers, and turned toward the door.

"One last thing," I said before leaving. "Is there any way you can figure out what had been on Marilyn Chase's mind about Roniece?"

The phone rang, and she answered it and began speaking in Spanish. She sounded cheerful and smiled while she talked. After hanging up, her distressed appearance returned once again.

"I'm sorry," she said. "Business never stops. I'm afraid the best chance of learning what was on Marilyn's mind is finding Roniece and getting her to tell the whole story."

"Yeah. Just hoping you might have some little clue."

We said our good-byes and I left her office. My wristwatch read 3:45 p.m. While still outside Juanita's door, I turned on my cell phone and checked for messages. Nothing. L.C. hadn't come up with anything yet. Or, maybe he had, and he couldn't call me. There were some things he might do that I wouldn't want to know about.

My footsteps echoed throughout the corridors of City Hall. The image of Juanita Velez reflected through my thoughts. It had been a long time since a woman had had that kind of effect on me. I decided to take the stairs down. I hoped to clear my mind by the time I reached the exit.

"I can't be distracted by a woman," I said while hopping down the stairs. My feelings continued wildly bounding like an unbroken stallion. I'd have to get my spurs on and break the sucker.

My mind went back to the "coincidence" of Roniece being with Marilyn Chase and running from the festival grounds, and Marilyn's sudden murder. That had to be a humdinger of a story.

Outside, the city was hot, hotter than I remembered when I'd arrived at City Hall. A blistering, desert-like wind blew at me while I walked through a corridor of tall office buildings toward my car. When I rounded a corner, the wind stopped, and the brutal summer sun began baking me. The old saying goes, "You could fry an egg on the sidewalk." Hell, I could have looked like a burnt bacon strip if I'd stayed too long in one place.

I thought how the weather conditions were like private detective work – you get blasted, you get fried, the wind blows. You subject yourself to the elements and plow ahead.

Had meeting Juanita Velez and swooning like an eighteen-year-old with testosterone pouring out like sweat caused me to think like a pseudo-intellectual horse's ass?

Yes.

I arrived at my car and slowly drove home. Juanita had provided some interesting information, especially about Roniece and the festival grounds, but there were no immediate deductions to be made. I was stuck waiting for L.C. to call and tell me about his day.

CHAPTER EIGHT

My cell phone rang while I walked from the underground garage up to my apartment. It felt like L.C.'s ring so, without checking the caller ID, I answered, "What up, bro'."

"You don't have the soul to talk like that, brother." It was L.C., sounding pleased about something.

"What's goin' on? You squeeze Elmore into a ball of glue?"

"Now what makes you think I'd do a thing like that?" he asked, laughing. "I didn't have to squeeze Elmore into no ball of glue, although he knew I could if I'd wanted to. I waited outside his joint until he drove up and went in, and I followed him. He talked faster than a Three-card Monte dealer. Must have been 'cause he was alone. He don't know Roniece well, but he knows our anonymous girl."

"Who is she? Where is she?"

"Calls herself 'Mina.' Lives at 2026 North 14th Street. I'm parked outside her house right now. Elmore says she should be here. Slide on over and we can knock on her door."

"She might be unhappy to see us."

"Tough shit."

I went back down to my car and drove to Mina's address. She lived in the heart of the inner city, in what has been euphemistically referred to as a "depressed neighborhood." Depressed didn't begin to describe the neighborhood. Words like forsaken, hopeless, beaten-to-death, were far more appropriate. The stifling summer heat forced people onto their porches, yards, and sidewalks outside their dilapidated homes.

L.C.'s car was parked several doors away from Mina's. I drove past her house, which was in better condition than the others – a freshly painted duplex that actually had a lawn in front instead of a dirt patch eroding onto the sidewalk, and no debris. Window air conditioners hummed in first and second floor windows of the house, the only air conditioners I saw on the block. No one was outside.

L.C. got out of his car while I parked on the street across from him. He smiled and said nothing when I got out and trotted up to join him. We walked together in silence, L.C.'s usual habit when he was on the move, like a crocodile zeroing in on its prey. When we approached her property, L.C. signaled me toward the back door while he hopped up the stairs to the front. I was the detective, I should have been in charge, but L.C. knew what he was doing. And he had a racial edge, if he needed to throw his weight around.

After a short wait at the back door in the blistering sun, L.C. called to me, "Hey Jack, come to the front." I walked fast to the porch and entered the front door, which L.C. held open for me. Inside, the scent of inexpensive perfume was strong. After walking through a short, dark hallway, I entered the living room, which was nearly as dark. One heavily shaded lamp was on, casting dim light. My eyes needed to adjust before I could see.

An extremely thick carpet cushioned each step. I gradually saw more. Before me in the corner of the room sat an extremely attractive black woman, with long straight black hair and showgirl makeup, dressed in scanty, sexy lingerie. The chair was wicker with a circular seat, a high back, and no armrests. She smiled and parted her bare legs ever so slightly.

I scanned the room. Behind me a double sofa covered in purple velour stood before a window covered by translucent sheers. A velour cornice on top and a thick, floor length over drapery parted by a gold cord with tasseled tiebacks, completed the treatment. The drapes matched the sofa. Before turning back to the woman and L.C., a cynical remark tried to be thought up in my mind and said. It never made it.

"This is Mina," L.C. said, while standing a couple feet away and pointing at her.

"Hi, Mina," I said. "Nice to meet you."

Mina smiled broadly at both of us, eyeing us up and down.

I waited for L.C. to make a move – this was his show all the way.

He gently took her hand and pulled her to her feet.

"We haven't talked our deal yet," she said coyly. By her husky voice I knew she was the one who'd called me about seeing me in Aquarius.

I couldn't believe she didn't recognize us, and I couldn't take the silly show any more. "How'd you get us in here?" I asked L.C.

"Elmore called from his club and told Mina here that I was lookin' for a girl, that he'd vouch for me and she didn't need no security. She told him I should come on over, and to bring my white friend. My foot was in the door before I even got here."

L.C. hadn't told me Mina was a prostitute – his little joke. Mina looked back and forth at us, obviously not understanding what was happening.

"For chrissakes, Mina," I said. "We were in Aquarius yesterday. Don't you remember us?"

She yanked her hand out of L.C.'s. "What's goin' on?" she shouted.

"I'm Jack Blanchard. This is L.C. Veasley. You called us both after you overheard me talking to Elmore Harris about L.C.'s sister, Roniece Veasley."

Her eyes widened, her jaw dropped. Her legs wobbled and she sat down hard. She squinted and looked hard at both of us, and slowly a look of recognition came over her face.

"Damn. It's too dark even for me in here. I'm gettin' to be a damn, greedy fool."

L.C. laughed. "You really couldn't remember us from yesterday?"

She sat back in her wicker chair and waved her arm around. "I see so many men everywhere, I can't remember where I seen everybody."

"Don't worry about it," I said. "I busted one lady of pleasure twice in three days when I was a vice cop."

She sighed disgustedly. "This ain't no bust." She pointed at me. "You not a cop. At least, you said you wasn't." She pointed at L.C. "And you and me never talked no sex or money." She folded her arms across her breasts and brought her legs up onto the chair to sit cross-legged.

"You're right," I said. "This ain't no bust."

"Couldn't remember me," L.C. muttered. "Everybody know me. Nobody forget me."

She snapped her fingers and sneered at him, and them pointed me. "I look at the white boys." She continued looking with disgust at L.C. "He cute. I'd do him for nothin,' brutha."

"I'm hurt," L.C. said. He motioned toward me dismissively. "White boy here draws all the attention to hisself."

"Sorry, honey," she said to L.C. "You don't make no big impression."

"You know why were here, Mina," I said. "Is that your real name . . .'Mina'?"

"I'm only a greedy fool. I ain't dumb. And my real name's Colette."

"Roniece's on the run, again," L.C. said. "I think she's in serious trouble."

Mina's body language softened. A little. She remained quiet while a skeptical look crossed her face. "What you want from me?"

I paused before asking questions. She wasn't gonna like them.

"Have you seen Roniece at all since she first left her mother's home last week?" I asked.

The smile vacuumed off her face. She remained silent.

"We need to know, Mina, or should I call you 'Colette'?"

She shifted in her chair. "Colette."

"I think Roniece's life may be at stake, the way she's acting. I think you might know why, or at least have some idea. And I think you know where we can find her."

She stood and reached for a robe on a wooden clothes rack behind her chair. Her smooth brown body was perfectly shaped, well toned yet voluptuous. She was built for sex. She put on her robe and sat down, then grabbed and lit a cigarette from a nearby end table. She remained silent. I could almost see icicles growing on her.

I had to push her. "If I was a cop, I could bring you in as a material witness on a possible homicide."

She sat bolt upright in her chair. "What homicide? Ain't nobody dead."

"Maybe Roniece's. How would you know she's not dead?"

She closed her eyes and sighed. She looked disgusted. "She made me promise I wouldn't say nothin'."

I pointed toward L.C. "L.C. here made me promise I'd find her. He gets mad when I break my promises. Real mad. Look at him. Between you and me, who do you think has more to fear?"

She shook her head slowly. "That girl been into somethin' way over her head."

"Do you know where she is?" I asked in a pleading tone.

"Not right now."

She was playing me, but I kept a patient front. "You're the one everyone thinks is her auntie. Right?"

"She my God cousin. I help her some. People in the 'hood make a turn about, sayin' I'm her 'auntie.' Shit."

I didn't understand. "God cousin? What's that?"

"It's street. We close to each other, close to God."

"They's kids playin,'" L.C. said. "They all call each other God cousin, God sister, God *everything*. They're all assholes who don't even know each other."

There was a long silence.

"I see," I said. "So then there's no blood relation?"

"No," Colette said softly.

"Is she hookin'?" L.C. asked loudly.

Colette and I both jumped. He glared at her, his hands balled into fists.

"Did you turn her out? 'Cause if you did—"

"L.C., cut it out!" I couldn't believe I'd yelled at him, but I had to shut him up. "There's more important things to consider right now."

A blank look immediately came over him and he relaxed his posture, leaning against a nearby fake fireplace mantle and crossing one foot in front of the other.

Colette shrank down into her chair, looking at us with wide eyes. "No," she said to L.C. "Roniece don't party. Never did, far as I know. I let her stay here sometimes. She has her own hustle."

L.C. said, "What hustle?—"

"L.C.," I said sharply. "This is my gig now. Let me work it."

He turned his eyes away and lowered his head.

"Listen," I said to Colette, "Does she come here when she's in trouble? Do you expect her to come now?"

"I don't know when she come. She in and out."

I didn't believe her. "When will you see her next?"

"I'm not sure." She looked at us with teary eyes. "She my friend. Has been since we was kids. She always look out for me. She ain't like no one else. She don't freeload and she don't steal."

I didn't want L.C. or me telling her too much. "It doesn't matter right now," I said. "Finding her and getting her to a safe place is all that counts." I dug into my pants pocket, pulled out my car keys and tossed them to L.C. I glanced at Colette, and then said, "I got a feeling Roniece's crashing here. I'm going to stay in case she shows up."

I waited a moment, but Colette said nothing.

"Roniece doesn't know my car," I said to L.C., "but park it on another block, anyway. Drive home and call a cab to come back." I turned to look at Colette. "We're gonna camp out here to see if Roniece comes around. You know L.C. ain't gonna let this go. This girl's gonna end up dead—"

"No, no," Colette said desperately, waving her arms in front of her. She slouched, looking sheepish. "I can't let you do all that."

She stood, looked at us while putting her forefinger to her lips signaling silence, and walked from the living room toward an outer hallway at the back of the house. She motioned for us to follow.

We went into the hallway and stood at the bottom of a staircase leading to a second floor residence. Colette walked up the stairs, each step creaking loudly, and knocked on the door at the top. "Roniece. Roniece, honey, open up." She turned back to L.C. and me. "She's afraid she could be found at the shelter or L.C.'s house."

A moment before I thought to have L.C. check outside, I saw Roniece through the rear door window climbing down a pole that supported an outdoor porch at the rear of the upper residence. She'd obviously heard us and decided to boogie while Colette climbed the stairs.

Apparently seeing her also, L.C. pushed me aside, stormed toward the door, and bolted outside. I followed, and the chase was on. Roniece ran and leaped with amazing speed and agility over cyclone and picket fences dividing some of the back yards. L.C. was even faster. I brought up the rear, losing ground with pathetic speed.

After leaping one fence, L.C. got stuck in a rose bush, the thorns hooking and tearing his pants. "Goddammit," he yelled while ripping himself free.

I cautiously crawled over the fence and ran past him. We were in trouble. Roniece was three backyards ahead and picking up speed. Sucking in air burned my lungs. A cold sweat broke on my skin. Suddenly, L.C. ran past me, hurdling the fences ahead. My running slowed to a tortured jog, but I continued following, climbing fence after fence.

I'd lost sight of them both. While stopping in a backyard and bending over, starry patterns sprinkled across my vision. I straightened and tried rejoining the chase, but my legs ignored my brain and refused to move. A moment later I saw the flash of two people colliding in a yard nearly a block ahead of me. A woman's scream pierced the air, followed by a man's unintelligible yelling. L.C. had caught Roniece.

She started screaming again, but an instant later all sounds stopped. L.C. had her by the arm and marched her into the alley. I could barely move, but managed to walk from the yard into the alley and joined them when L.C. brought her to where I stood. We all proceeded back to Colette's house.

A malnourished, brown and white, shorthaired dog approached us seemingly from nowhere, and then backed away. A few ramshackle garages stood with their overhead doors gone and the insides piled high with auto scrap and other junk. One yard had the remnants of three rusted, stripped cars that looked as though they'd been there for years.

"We're goin' back upstairs, and we're gonna talk," L.C. said in a low, angry growl. He held Roniece tightly by the arm while continued walking toward Colette's house.

Roniece said nothing, looking defiant and about to cry.

I wiped the sweat from my face and arms with my hands. My breathing was hot and rapid, and my heart slugged away in my chest.

My stomach had begun to turn, and I tried sweet-talking it in my thoughts. I got no response, but felt grateful I hadn't been answered with a bolt of vomit spewing up my gullet.

When we got to Colette's rear door she let us in and L.C. hustled Roniece up the rear stairs. She slipped and fell, and L.C. dragged her to her feet. Colette had a frightened look on her face.

"It will be dark pretty soon, and we'll get her out of here," I said to Colette, trying to reassure her.

"I'm worried about her," Colette said. "She's afraid for her life."

"You're a good friend, but sometimes we can't give our friends the help they need."

She brought a burning cigarette with a trembling hand to her lips and gave me a sad look. "Take care of her," she said, then turned and walked back into her house.

I went upstairs.

CHAPTER NINE

L.C. and Roniece sat together on a dark cloth couch in the sparsely furnished living room of the apartment above Colette's. Next to the couch sat a badly scratched, cheaply made end table, upon which was an even cheaper table lamp. An old, beat up TV with a filthy screen sat in one corner.

The sheer curtains covering the tall windows behind the couch were drawn, allowing diffuse light into the room. An air conditioner blasted away in the adjacent dining room window. I stood beneath the archway separating the rooms, feeling awkward.

We were all still panting. My sweat-soaked shirt rapidly chilled from the air conditioning. I went into the kitchen, grabbed a chair, and brought it to the living room, then turned it around and sat with my arms folded over the back. L.C. looked at me expectantly, while Roniece held her gaze on the floor.

I breathed deeply and blew out the air. "Okay, from the beginning. What the heck is going on?"

Roniece said nothing, parted her lips and moistened them with her tongue. Her face flushed. She sniffed deeply and began softly crying. L.C. moved closer to her and she fell into his arms. He cradled her head and stroked her hair.

"It's okay, baby," he said softly, repeatedly.

While waiting, I looked around the living room, back to the dining room and the kitchen beyond. The place was reasonably clean – not the usual shit hole of someone on the pipe. I took it as a sign that she really was clean. Maybe Colette had been helping her keep it up. I looked back at L.C., with my eyebrows raised. He nodded.

I looked back at Roniece. "Roniece, we can only help you if you tell us what's going on."

She snuffled and pulled her head up from L.C.'s shoulder. She'd stopped crying. L.C. handed her a tissue box from the end table.

"Someone out to kill me," she said, and blew her nose. "Might be the Mafia."

I stifled a laugh. "The *Mafia*?" Jesus, she thought L.C. and I were stupid. "Why would the Mafia be after you?" I asked in as sincere a voice as I could muster.

"Drugs."

It was a start. A weak one, but a start.

"Anything specific?" I asked, forcing a gentle tone that I worried sounded like rank condescension. "Like who, and when, and all that stuff?"

"From a while ago."

It would be tough sledding with her all the way.

"Roniece," I said, "L.C. and I know more than you think. You should try opening up."

"I think they was supplyin' Jones and them with dope. Somethin' went wrong, an' they kill't all them in the car. I works for Jones then, and they been after me ever since."

I looked at L.C., who sat in silence, a despairing look on his face. He slowly shook his head.

"The Mafia was supplying Earl with dope?" I said.

"Uh-huh."

"Why would they be after you, now?"

She waved her hand at me.

"Okay. And this was 'a while ago'? How long?"

Her jaw tightened. She squeezed her lips flat and remained silent.

"I believe you. Someone wants to kill you over drugs. But you've got to be more specific." Like telling the damn truth.

She turned her face from me, refusing to speak. L.C. tried rubbing her back, but she jerked away.

I waited for a long moment. "So, how about it?"

She turned her head farther way. Her jaw muscles throbbed.

"I think crazy Reggie's story is looking pretty good," I said. "You know somethin' more, a lot more, an' you're still on a list to be killed. But the last part, you know."

She still didn't move.

"I think you know who killed Jones and the others."

She slowly turned her head toward me. "I don't know nothin' 'bout who killed 'em." Her lower jaw trembled. Tears bulged in her eyes.

"But you did work for Jones, along with Reggie. And you believe the same person who killed Jones and all them is still after you, even two years later." I paused. "As I said, I believe you know who it is."

She turned her head away and snorted.

"The Mafia's not after you," I said.

"May as well *be* Mafia. Ain' nobody can help. Ain' no escape."

It was time for a change of pace. "Why did you tell your mother you worked at a car wash after you got off crack, and not City Hall?"

L.C. looked at me with a shocked expression. "What the hell . . . ?"

Roniece remained still and silent.

"Why did you run from the Summerfest grounds last week?" I asked.

L.C. quickly looked at her, then back at me, his eyes bulging.

A tortured, helpless look crossed Roniece's face. She looked at L.C., then back at me. "That don't have nothin' to do with this."

"I believe your running from the festival grounds has everything to do with it," I said. "From there you went missing for five days. You're scared to death. What makes you think—"

She stood. "Fuck you, motherfucker!" She began crying again. She turned and walked to the end of the couch.

"We're going nowhere, L.C."

L.C. still looked shocked. "What's all this about Roniece workin' at City Hall, and runnin' from the festival grounds?"

"I got a call from Juanita Velez, head of Social Services. Roniece worked directly for her. I meant to tell you when you called, but the Mina hooker show was starting and I got distracted."

L.C. stood. He rubbed both hands over his scalp. His skin had paled and gone dry. He walked toward Roniece.

"What the fuck is going on, girl?" he shouted.

She stood with her back to him. She started trembling.

L.C. stopped before reaching her, and looked at me. "What's all this City Hall bullshit?" He looked back at Roniece, still standing with her back to him. "An' what you doin' at the Summerfest grounds? An' runnin'. Runnin' from what?" He reached out and grabbed a hank of her hair. "You tell us what happened, goddamn it."

She screamed, clamped both her hands on his, and tried twisting away from him. He pulled her to her knees and raised one hand as though to strike her.

"L.C.," I said, quickly getting off my chair and grabbing his arm. He offered no resistance, and meekly let his hand drop to his side. He let go of her hair. She remained kneeling, covered her face with her hands, and sobbed even harder.

"Where'd you get all this, man?" L.C. said, staring at me, disbelieving. "City Hall. The festival grounds. And *when*?"

"This afternoon. Just before you called about Mina. Or Colette."

We remained standing, waiting for Roniece to compose herself. After a moment, L.C. stooped and gently grabbed Roniece by the waist and pulled her to her feet. They returned to their places on the couch, and I sat once again on the kitchen chair.

"Roniece," I said, "you *know* how I found out about City Hall and the festival. I think you ran because you saw someone from your drug days that you're scared to death of."

Roniece stopped crying. "Think what you want."

"This won't go away just because you don't talk about it. Cancers don't stop growing by ignoring them."

Resignedly, she drew in a deep breath and blew it out. "Reggie said some black dude killed 'em all." She sighed and said, almost whimsically, "I think the Mafia behind it."

L.C. and I looked at each other, our collective patience long gone.

Follow every rabbit down every hole, I reminded myself. I calmly asked, "How would Reggie know a black guy did it? And why do you insist that the Mafia's involved?"

"I guess he hear from the street. The street know a lot. And I – I think the Mafia behind it." She repeated her Mafia claim the way a defiant child tries irritating its parents.

I paused. Being a schizophrenic, Reggie couldn't be trusted not to have been relating his own delusions to her. Of course, given her terror, Roniece could have been making up a story to throw me off.

"Do you trust Reggie to tell you the truth?" I asked.

She grunted. "A couple weeks after Earl Jones was murdered, Reggie shoots two dudes, an' goes to jail. Everybody say it connected to Earl. Reggie know somethin'."

Yeah, he knew something. "Reggie has been considered a suspect in the killings." Of course, I hadn't known that for a fact. "What do you think?"

She fidgeted, repositioned herself in her seat, and said, "Reggie didn't ambush nobody. Reggie couldn't plan a barbecue."

She was still lying about Reggie, but then I believed she was lying about most everything.

After a long moment, I said, "How about it, Roniece? Why'd you run and hide last week?"

She looked up at me sharply. "I felt like it."

"How about Kim Artic, Earl Jones's girlfriend who was murdered with him? I heard you knew her – were good friends with her."

"Everybody from the neighborhood knew her 'cuz she a councilman's daughter. That's all."

Denials and short-stroked explanations. It felt hopeless.

I looked at L.C. "I don't know what else we can do." I turned to her. "You know more, a lot more. Your Mafia story is silly crap. But something is very wrong and if you're in the trouble I think you may be in, and your plan is to keep running, you'll end up dead."

She sat back and folded arms over her lap. She still looked away. A large tear slipped down her cheek.

"One last thing," I said. "You were at the festival grounds with Marilyn Chase before you went on the run. Don't bother denying it."

She looked me straight in the eye. "So what?"

"How did you get involved with Marilyn Chase, for chrissakes?" L.C. shouted, a look of intense disbelief returning to his face. One more rapid change and his face would twist right off.

"Later, L.C." I said.

He sat back, rolled his eyes upward and shook his head.

Roniece still looked hard at me. "You think there a hook up?"

"With what?"

She made a disgusted look and shut her eyes. "You playin' games. Why you bring her up?"

"Well, with you dodging death and all, and Marilyn being murdered so soon after you ran—"

"The mayor did it, motherfucker! Ask the newspapers."

"Okay. Okay." I put my hands up. "The mayor did it."

"Good God, girl," L.C. said. "You got around, didn't you?"

"You got around your own self."

"All right, all right," I said, ending their brewing spat. "Everybody did everything. Let's cool it."

Roniece lowered her chin toward her chest and began chewing on a fingernail. She was completely shutting down. She was getting ready to tell me to go bite a dead dog in the ass. I'd learned long ago not to read into things, and not to let wild-ass theories crop up. But Roniece had jumped through too many hoops to get away from something. She was too terrified. It made sense that Four Dead had told at least some truth about her fears, as far as he was able. And it added more credibility to Juanita's hunch about Marilyn Chase.

"I think we should give it a rest," I said. I looked at Roniece. "Are you going to stay close, or run again?"

"She can stay with me until she settles down," L.C. said. "I'll take her home when we leave."

I stood and excused myself, leaving L.C. and Roniece sitting quietly in the living room. I went to my car and drove toward home. Four Dead told the truth when he said that a black guy killed Earl Jones and the others. The police report might give me a hint when I finally read it. I wasn't too hopeful. The inner city underworld being the tricky place it is, Four Dead could have learned about it a hundred ways.

But, anything can happen. Sometimes a young child can describe every detail of a dope house operation, when people are there, even provide names. They can start the break-up of a major drug gang by having a friendly conversation with a cop in a neighborhood patrol car.

I know, because a youngster did that for me – and his neighborhood – when I was a patrol officer, back in the day.

Whatever else, Roniece's missing case had been solved. Twice. Sure, she'd come home on her own once, and L.C. got the address where she turned out to be hiding the next time, but I figured I'd applied the pressure to make it all happen. Or something like that. That's why L.C. had hired me – to find Roniece – not to investigate any murders. I couldn't stick my nose into a two-year-old cold-case homicide, or take on the Mafia. Could I?

Sure, I could. I had nothing more pressing to do, and I was curious as hell. And, I could handle Roniece's Mafia claim – especially since there was nothing to it. The odds were extremely against me figuring anything out, but I'd faced that before and beat the bushes anyway.

It was late, past nine o'clock, when I arrived at my apartment. I relished my plans for the following day – call Juanita Velez about Roniece, maybe get to see Juanita again, and set up another interview with Four Dead at the state penitentiary.

CHAPTER TEN

Juanita Velez wasn't in her office when I first called at 8:30 a.m., so I left my name and number on her voice mail. I sat at my kitchen table, reading the newspaper, not surprised that there was nothing new about Marilyn Chase's murder. The coffee I'd brewed tasted good. The caffeine stoked me up. Three faxes from clients lay in my machine. They were all requests from defense attorneys for files and records. They could wait.

I was looking forward to my visit with Four Dead. That was, if he would still to talk to me. I called the prison and spoke with a clerk who said there shouldn't be any problem – I had been his only visitor in the 18 months he'd been there. A minute later she confirmed my appointment with him. I looked forward again to the drive's pleasant diversion.

The phone rang.

"How you doin'?"

It was L.C. "I want to take you out to dinner tonight, for everything you've done."

"You paid me, more than my usual fee, and now I get dinner? I should be taking you out."

"Don't argue, or I'll squeeze you into a ball of glue." He laughed.

"I'd be happy to go to dinner. The steak joint on Juneau Avenue again?"

"You got it."

An incoming call signaled, and I hung up with L.C. to answer it.

"Mr. Blanchard?" It was Juanita Velez, sounding grave.

I didn't acknowledge her tone. "Hello, Ms. Velez. How are you?"

"I'm good."

"Please. Call me Jack."

"All right, Jack. I'm calling about Roniece. Is there anything new?"

She didn't tell me to call her Juanita, which was disappointing, but then she didn't sound in a social mood. "Yes, there is. We found her last night, she's safe and sound."

"That's good. That's wonderful. Please tell her to call me. And I'd like to speak with you again soon, but I'd rather do it in person."

She said 3:00 p.m. in her office would be good once again. I agreed to be there and hung up.

The drive to the prison wasn't as enjoyable as I'd hoped. Juanita had been too serious during our phone conversation, and I was concerned. The time passed slowly, but eventually I found myself in the same depressing prison visiting stall where I'd been the last time I talked to Four Dead. This time, I'd arrived first. It had been less than a week since I'd been there, but it seemed like forever.

As I drummed my fingers impatiently on the ledge before me, my anxiety rose. This interview was more important to me than I'd thought. Despite my doubts about Four Dead, I felt he could possibly shed more light on the murder of Earl Jones and his bunch – and perhaps move me closer to the whole story about Roniece. In turn, that could possibly provide clues about Marilyn Chase's murder. I kept in mind that it was all a major stretch, and that I'd had similar feelings many times while investigating homicides as a police detective, only to have the cases die and be buried in the files, never to be exhumed.

A heavy steel door scraping its runner sounded from the end of the hall beyond the bulletproof windows. A moment later the door slammed against a doorpost. The sound of footsteps and the rattling of prisoners' chains came toward me. I grew more anxious.

"I knew you'd be back," Four Dead said contemptuously while a guard walked him to the stool opposite the Plexiglas window and me. He seemed sharper than the last time I saw him.

"Can't find Roniece," he taunted. He must have spit his last dose of Thorazine. "Need more clues, right?" His voice was strong, his sarcastic glee unrestrained.

"So, how's life?" I asked in an equally sarcastic tone. I stopped myself. I needed his cooperation.

"Same as last time. Time don't move when you jailin'.'"

He sat straight, smiling. Despite his agitation, he was talkative, maybe cooperative. I decided to play along and not tell him that Roniece had been located. "I'm still strugglin', Four D. I mean, Four Dead. There's things I need to know."

His smile broadened. "Can't find a nigga' in a woodpile." He laughed and bent forward, clapping his hands.

"I thought the N-word was offensive, that my spine would curve and my brain would explode just by hearing it."

He ignored me and continued giggling. "She slippery. She cool."

"You seem full of energy. You stop takin' your meds?"

He stopped and looked at me, slowly losing his smile. I'd chanced alienating him, but I wanted him serious.

"Don't worry," he said without any sign of feeling offended. "I got control."

A half dozen remarks died on my tongue before I opened my mouth to speak. Then, I said, "Maybe you can help me with some stuff."

He had the satisfied look of a fat man after eating Thanksgiving dinner. "Maybe. Maybe not."

"Along the way I heard that you said a black man had shot Earl Jones and the others. How do you know that?"

His pleased look fell away. His bug eyes narrowed. "Who tell you 'dat?"

"More than one person," I said, lying through my teeth. "Some say you said it. Others think you were somehow involved."

He looked at me sharply. "What it got to do with Roniece?"

"Maybe nothing, maybe everything. You know what she's afraid of."

His eyes grew dull, as though life itself were leaving his body. He morphed in and out of lucidity with astonishing speed. His mental state was flimsier than a politician's promise. He motioned upward with his hand, and then looked up at the ceiling. He cocked his head, as though he were straining to hear someone speak. I waited, watching while he dropped his hand to his lap and leveled his eyes at me.

He had a strange, far-off stare, as though he'd gone through a looking glass and was trying to look back at me. He made a small smile, a smile that seemed to come from someone else's face.

"I got it all in here," he said while raising a finger to his head and tapping his temple. "It all in here, and nobody can have it."

My heart sank. His delusions had apparently stepped in to protect him. I'd dealt with schizophrenics before – that's a common thing with them, especially if they've been erratic in taking their medication. It looked as though I'd never get anything meaningful from him.

"I'm glad for you, Four Dead."

"It dark in the alley," he said. "I walks all aroun' the 'hood. Musta waited a hour."

I sat very still, looking away from him. I couldn't believe what I'd heard. I didn't know if I should let him ramble with what sounded like a wild story, or try asking questions.

"I gots my 'nine' up under my jacket, 'case things go bad. Car drives up an' I crosses the alley an' hides next to a garage. I looks up and the shootin' starts – jus' like 'dat. I start shakin'. I lays down flat. At first, I don' see nobody – jus' a Uzi flashin', or somethin'. The flashes light up the dude holding the shit. He all in black, lookin' like a damn ninja. The fire." He paused and looked at me. "The fire look pretty." He looked down and began talking again. "The noise. I pisses where I lay. The car shakin' when it gets hit. Thought it wouldn' never stop."

He stopped talking. I felt my eyes growing big. The chill that started in my spine leaped to my throat. He sat slumping on his stool, his eyes glazed over and staring, as though he were watching the scene he'd described again and again.

"I tells it to some dudes in here," he said in a dull voice while sweeping his arm around and looking back at me. "They see my tattoo. Some figure I done it. Who the fuck write a murder confession on they own arm? I ain't crazy. Now everybody know what I say, but nobody know what I'm talkin' 'bout."

"You, ah . . ." I said, but stopped to clear my throat. "You've told people about this – here – in this prison? And now, everybody knows?"

"Uh-huh. It go aroun' on a humbug. Gets to everybody, sooner or later."

"Were you there? You saw the shooting?"

"Be in my head, 'dat the only place I count. 'Four Dead, In My Head.' 'Dat what I call it."

"Did you make it up? Did you just hear about it?"

He seemed to be rallying and smiled again – a focused, wry smile. "Nobody know. Nobody care."

Some of what he'd said about the shooting had been made public – the victims were together in the car, which had been riddled with bullets. What he claimed were his personal observations had yet to be verified – the car pulling into the alley, the flashing Uzi lighting up a black shooter who'd resembled a "ninja." Four Dead had worked for Earl Jones – had been a dope runner, a server at dope houses. It was plausible that Jones had had a meeting that night in the alley and that he had been Jones's lookout. Roniece had said there was bad blood between Earl and – and the *Mafia,* as I recalled.

Yeah, Four Dead could have been a lookout. Chances were he'd been there.

He talked on, digressing to himself. "It in my head. It mine now. 'Four Dead, In My Head.'"

I decided to push him. "You *were* there, weren't you, Four Dead?"

"I'm in my head, man. 'Dat all I count."

"How else could you have this scene in your head? And why would you call yourself 'Four Dead?' It's no coincidence four people were killed. Why else would you tattoo that name on your arm?"

"I seen lots a things. It all run together."

I wanted to keep him talking, hoping to catch him spilling a crucial, verifiable detail. "The black guy who shot them all. Did you see his face?"

"Ha, ha. He don't have no face. He all black."

I took a different tack. "Are you saying no one in the prison believed your story?"

"My lawyer calls a year ago. Says the po-lice wants to talk wid' me 'bout it. He say somebody told."

"Did you talk to the police?"

"Uh-uh. I don' be talkin' to no po-po."

It figured. My hot bit of new insight was old news. I should have known better than to get excited. I'd check later to see what the cops knew about Four Dead. They wouldn't be anxious to talk to him anyway, loon that he was. If he'd witnessed the shooting – and I wasn't sure he hadn't – the way he'd been telling the story was next to worthless, in a strictly legal sense. He could have made up the lone black "ninja" shooter.

Shit.

I decided to try again. "Was it Earl Jones, and everyone, you saw get shot?"

His eyes lit up like a fisherman reeling in a big one. "All 'dat lef' is in my head. 'Dat all I count."

All he counted was a vision of a horrible murder. Maybe a memory, probably not.

"Is it like a film you play in your mind?" I asked.

"Sometimes. Sometimes a picture. A lot o' pictures."

He seemed proud and amused. I could tell that conjuring up the shooting image gave him pleasure. It was unlikely that he'd ever fly too close to the flame – that he'd ever give the details necessary to prove he'd seen Earl Jones and the others get shot. *Four Dead, In My Head*, he called it. His very own, private portrait of a human slaughter hanging in his crazy house of a mind.

I switched tacks again. "And the shooting you were involved with two weeks later, where you killed those guys . . ."

"Comes up behind me on the street and say, 'y'all brake yourself,' like they's doin' a robbery." He'd segued quickly and smoothly to that story. The visuals of that shooting probably hung in his mind next to the *Four Dead* portrait.

He'd begun returning to the alert state he'd been in when our visit had begun. I decided to let him talk, even though I already knew everything I'd cared to know about his own murder case. Still, maybe he'd say something useful.

"I turns an' looks," he continued. "I knows 'em – they was Earl's other dope dealers - and they knows me. They was three of 'em. One of 'em starts laughin'. The others, they stay serious. I runs and they shoots. I turn an' pulls my shit and shoots back. We runs an' trades shots all aroun' the 'hood. When it stop, two of 'em was dead. The other dude – who laughs – he runs."

"Was one of them the guy who shot Earl?" I asked, hoping to catch him out. "You know, trying to eliminate the competition?"

He waved his hand. "They was Earl's guys. They'd have sucked his dick."

"And the police didn't buy your robbery and self-defense story?"

He laughed. "Naw. They checks our sheets and sees we was – sees me an' 'dem hung around."

"You'd been associates."

"Yeah. Associates. Been arrested together. Shit like 'dat."

I sat silently for a while. I had to accept that Four Dead wasn't going to tell me anything directly helpful. Useful for further investigation. Perhaps. But if he *had* been an eyewitness to the Jones shooting – and I was starting to think more yes than no – he almost certainly couldn't ID the killer. If he could, he'd have done so already. Crazy or not, he'd have been sharp enough to belly up and get himself a break on his own case.

"Well, Four D, once again I gotta go. It was nice hearing about the photograph you have in your head. Maybe someday I can have an autographed copy."

After standing, I stopped to watch the guards take him away. Whacked out and witless though he was, the little sucker had gotten to me. My only consolation was that he had no idea he'd done it. But it was small consolation – very small.

While leaving, I comforted myself with my own words – there's no such thing as a bad hunch. But you feel sick when good hunches – things you know are the truth – don't pan out. This felt like one of those times. I'd felt sicker than this with other cases – there was one cop killing we never pinned on the shooter. I tried comforting myself again. It didn't work.

The interview with Four Dead had taken longer than I'd thought and I had to race to get to Juanita Velez's office on time. On the way back to town my thoughts changed from my disappointment over Four Dead to dread over what Juanita would have to say.

Once in her office, we exchanged perfunctory greetings and I sat down. She wore a fitted sleeveless black top and a knee-length teal skirt, revealing her shapely body. She went to her chair behind her desk and sat down. The sun wasn't as bright as the other day – the room wasn't as illuminated as then.

Large and intense, her soft brown eyes focused on me with a sweet, paralyzing sting. Her full lips and golden brown skin gave her a breathtaking sensuality. Her dark, shiny hair flowed down her chest, draping over her full breasts. She looked even more beautiful than the last time I'd seen her. My heartbeat took off on its own, hammering away at high speed inside my chest. My throat went dry.

"The detectives have been here, talking to everyone about Marilyn," she said without any preliminary discussion. "They talked to me, and I said I didn't know anything." She looked worried. "But I think I do know something."

The heady atmosphere had broken my concentration, but I recovered when she said those words. I braced myself. "Like what?"

"That Marilyn was on to something about Roniece, and what happened at the festival grounds. I don't know what, or how it would be relevant to her death." She was sitting rigidly, her forearms leaning on the edge of her desk. "I need your advice. I'll pay you."

I smiled and waved my hand. "No fee. Do you think what Marilyn was looking into about Roniece has something to do with her murder, Ms. Velez?"

She let out a heavy sigh. "Oh, please. It's Juanita. Call me Juanita."

A thrill went through me. Selfish bastard. It wasn't time for such an indulgence.

"And no," she continued, "I can't say that. But the police might want to know about it. They might think it does."

"Are you worried the police will be angry if they find out you didn't tell them what you know?"

"Maybe. For all I know they might think I'm hiding something. I got nervous and called you."

"Based on what you've told me, there's nothing that would interest the cops. If I were you, I'd only call them if I learned something I thought would be important to them. Besides, they're looking at the mayor as their suspect. Everyone knows that."

"I know, but no one here believes he did it. No one has any idea who might have."

"Does anyone here know any details? You know, when and where Marilyn was last seen alive? What's the mayor's alibi? The papers haven't given a hint of anything."

"No one's said anything to me."

She looked relieved and sat back in her chair. "Thanks." After a moment she said, "Now that the police are done searching, I've been asked to help go through Marilyn's office. I'll look for any notes, or whatever, that she may have left relating to Roniece. Things happened fast, though, and I'm not too hopeful."

"If you do find something, give me a call."

"I was planning on it. Do you have any ideas on what I should look for?"

"Things about people working at City Hall. It could be anything – vague notes to herself, office extension numbers. And it could be located anywhere in her office. It may not be obvious. Don't discount anyone as a possibility if you come across something. Even the mayor."

"I'll recover anything that even might seem important."

"I know you will. Was there any other talk about Kim Artic and her father? Anyone figure he was involved with drugs, too?"

"Some people here mentioned the possibility, but I always thought they were being vicious. Mr. Artic is a good man."

"So I've heard. By the way, I've been interviewing a convict – calls himself 'Four Dead' – at the state penitentiary who knows Roniece, and who knew Kim Artic. From a whole different point of view than yours, quite obviously. Weird though it may sound, he may eventually be of help. I'll try to coordinate any information you get with him, to see if he can pour some grease on any fires you might be able to start."

She smiled. "That would be unexpected. And, *Four Dead*? What sort of name is that?"

"That's a long, unimportant story – at least at this time." After a pause, I asked, "What do you think Marilyn suspected? How could Roniece have been hooked up?"

"Marilyn always played her cards close, never shared what she might have discovered. It's very possible that she took whatever she knew to her grave." She sighed and folded her arms in front across her chest.

"If there is a connection between Roniece running from the festival grounds and Marilyn's death – and that's still an unimaginable leap – at must involve someone at City Hall," I said.

There were still too many missing puzzle pieces to draw any inferences, let alone conclusions. I was just tossing ideas around to see if anything shook loose.

"What Marilyn knew may have involved the mayor, after all," I said. "You know that, don't you?" I didn't wait for her to answer. "That might have been part of the big scandal she mentioned – and the motive for killing her."

"I know. But I don't know what the scandal could be."

"Maybe the drug thing, with Artic and Roniece somehow connected. There would be large amounts of drug money."

Juanita slapped the desk with her hand. "I don't believe the mayor killed Marilyn Chase," she said angrily. "And Hayward Artic is not involved with drugs. And the mayor couldn't have been involved in something so lowlife as drug dealing – nor murdering the woman he loves when she found him out." A tear ran down her cheek. "It simply can't be true."

I didn't like it either. It was too bizarre. He would have killed his girlfriend for the usual motive. Without hearing a word on the police investigation, I still had to believe that Mayor McCord was their number one suspect. I assumed Marilyn hadn't had time to dig into the Roniece Veasley aspect of things. Still, something cold and prickly spun in my guts. At that moment I wished I were still a cop, just to know the inside story.

"I'm sorry if I was insensitive," I said. "I'm just considering all possibilities. It's a habit from my job."

She waved her hand. "Oh, I know. Every possibility has to be considered. You're just being a good detective."

Someone knocked on her door. She looked surprised. I turned back to look and the door opened without Juanita inviting anyone in. A man's head poked in, with the door still mostly closed. I recognized the full face with a dark mustache from Mayor McCord's press conference announcing Marilyn Chase's death – it was Vincent Dragos, Mayor McCord's police detective bodyguard.

CHAPTER ELEVEN

Dragos stood in the doorway for a moment, then said, "Hi, how ya' doin,' Juanita?" a little too casually.

Juanita didn't ask him in. He stepped inside anyway. His six-foot frame was cloaked with an inexpensive pinstriped gray suit that fit a little too tightly, outlining his muscular build. Walking directly to her desk, he pointedly ignored me. But I felt him measuring me with his peripheral vision.

Juanita was obviously displeased with his entrance. He obviously didn't give a damn.

"I heard the detectives on Marilyn's case have talked to you, like they did everyone else in City Hall," he said.

After an uneasy silence Juanita curtly said, "That's right."

He ignored her reaction and the chilled atmosphere in the room. "I'll be available as a liaison between everyone at City Hall and the police department. If there's anything I can do, answer any questions or whatever, get in touch with me. Okay?"

"Okay, Detective," she said softly.

His body language and facial expression showed that he either didn't recognize her coolness toward him, or didn't care. He seemed the type to be chronically unconcerned with other people's feelings. Maybe his job had made him jaded and a jerk – police work does that to some people. He had the officious, pushy way of a cop who'd either lost touch with the rest of the world, or who'd never had it.

He glanced over at me. He quickly looked away, then back.

"This is Jack Blanchard," Juanita said, introducing me unenthusiastically. She was forcing herself to be polite.

He turned toward me, stooped as though he were a school principal addressing a kindergartner, and stuck out his hand. A broad, phony smile stretched his lips – his eyes remained cool. He was smart and slick, and oppressive in his manner – good for interrogating prisoners, not good in social situations. I reached my hand toward his and we shook. He squeezed my hand overly hard.

"Name's Vincent Dragos," he said. "I'm a City Police Detective, assigned to the mayor's office."

"I'm a PI." I pulled my hand back and rubbed my fingers.

His eyes widened. "Really?" he said, sarcasm in his voice. "What are you working on?"

I was certain he'd somehow heard I'd been in Juanita's office at that time. I wondered if he moonlighted as a used car salesman. Or a politician.

"Nothing right now. I'm just discussing a personal matter with Juanita."

He stiffened and pulled away. He arched an eyebrow while hardening his look. He didn't like me coming onto his turf and speaking privately with a City Hall executive – not with even the slight possibility that I was somehow checking into the mayor's murder case, which he certainly suspected. He didn't like that I wouldn't tell him the nature of my business with Juanita Velez.

No doubt he didn't like PI's – the way cops usually feel, often with good reason. Too many PIs were flakes who screwed things up and were still paid exorbitantly by unsuspecting clients. But some were former and current cops who knew the score, while others came straight from the private sector and were exceedingly sharp. He didn't know my history or me, and I wanted to keep it that way.

He looked at Juanita and seemed to be expecting her to tell him why I was there. Another awkward silence followed.

"Well, just stopping by to touch bases," he said to her and turned to walk out.

"Nice meeting you," I said, while he walked past me.

"Yeah." He opened the door and stepped through the doorway. He stopped, backed into the office, and looked at me. "Could I see you out here?" he said, motioning to the hallway outside. It was not a request.

I stepped into the hallway, expecting him to bully me. I wasn't disappointed. After closing the door he stepped up to me, standing only inches away. It was a classic police tactic of invading someone's space to gain control – to annoy and intimidate. He seemed like someone who'd spent excessive time as a cop in the hard-core mean streets. I couldn't help smiling. He couldn't help bumping my chest with his shoulder.

"You're not looking into the Marilyn Chase matter, are you?"

He caught me off guard. He knew a PI wouldn't dare insert himself into a police homicide investigation, although that's what I was doing. He shouldn't have even thought to ask. I stepped backward. He stepped toward me.

"Why would you think that?" I asked, smiling as broadly as I could while he remained deep in my personal space.

He fumed. "Sometimes geeks in the PI world start nosing around a big case. You know, talking to witnesses on the sly, hoping they can solve it and make a name for themselves. That don't fly in this town. This ain't New York or L.A. This ain't a Hollywood movie. Capice?"

"Are you always this brash?"

The growing red tint on his face grew faster. "I don't like people interfering with a police investigation – especially a murder. And I speak for the entire department. You go too far and you'll be in a heap of trouble."

"You didn't answer my first question. Why do you think I'm investigating Ms. Chase's murder?" I paused, savoring the moment before saying my next words. "Well, of course, I'm not. As I said, I'm here on a private matter between Juanita and I."

He stepped back, looking surprised. The PI "geeks" he'd normally have dealt with would have been near tears and run from him. I curled my lip and snorted, and stepped toward Juanita's office door. He didn't move, forcing me to brush past him.

"Excuse me, Detective Dragos. I have to finish my business."

"What's your name, again?"

I took a business card out of my shirt pocket. "Here," I said, sticking the card in his hand. "I investigate all kinds of cases." Without looking back, I reentered Juanita's office.

"I don't believe we were finished," I said to her offhandedly while I went back to my chair.

"Detective Dragos has never been in my office before," Juanita said, looking puzzled. "Months will go by and I won't even see him."

"I'm sure he heard about me and is guarding his turf. He's also the mayor's man and keeps tabs on things."

"He's the mayor's lap dog. He's more of a valet than a body guard."

"He does more than protect and serve?"

"I've heard he tells the mayor what's going on in the police department. And anything else he thinks the mayor might like to know."

"He's a weasel."

"That's a good word."

"He's protecting his cushy assignment," I said. "This is a gravy job, with lots of perks and overtime. He could be transferred back to the street at any time."

"How do you know all that?"

I'd never mentioned my past to her. "I'm a former cop. A detective."

"Really? That's why you seem so in control. So experienced."

I suppressed a laugh. "I control nothing, and my experience has come by way of mistakes and hard lessons. I just mosey along, doing what I can."

She smiled. "You seem in control of yourself, and being experienced is good, no matter how you got it."

"Touché."

I wanted to get off the subject. "So, you don't often see Vincent Dragos? I suppose he's always with the mayor."

"Either that, or parading around the building, intimidating people. He's a jerk."

"How long has he been at City Hall?"

"A couple years. I've heard he worked on the Narcotics Squad before that, and had been on the Tactical Squad before he became a detective."

I'd worked on the Tac Squad, too. That assignment is mean streets plus. Being a narc only adds more layers to a cop's calluses.

"That kind of explains him," I said. "Not that it excuses him. His career path has been akin to attending the Saddam Hussein School of Charm. But you don't want a sheepskin from there, you want to be learning what *not* to do along those lines."

She looked thoughtful. "I'd never thought of it that way."

Who would, besides a cop?

I'd seen lots of guys like Dragos – the type who'd stepped on plenty of toes but managed to advance himself anyway. He'd learned how to bully effectively, and had everyone in City Hall bamboozled. His turn would come, and he'd be shocked to watch the steel reinforced concrete structure he thought he'd built turn into a house of cards.

"Do you think you'll hear from Roniece, again?" I asked.

"I hope so. I want to help."

"What would you say to her?"

"I'd ask if she wants to come back to work."

I was skeptical. Roniece seemed to need more time away from her problems before she was ready for the responsibilities of a job at City Hall.

"Is there anything more?" I asked.

"Not right now. I'll check Marilyn's office when I can, and I'll call you."

"Good." Smiling, I asked, "Are you sure you wouldn't rather tell the good City Hall detective . . .?"

"No, I wouldn't." She smiled back.

"Understood. I was kidding."

"I know, and I need a little humor right now." She continued smiling.

I stood. "I, ah, I guess I'll be going, then."

She stood also. "I'll go with you downstairs, if you don't mind. I need to walk off some tension."

Together we went into the hallway. A small breeze swept through the large, open corridor, wafting Juanita's scent to me. She smelled heavenly. We walked silently at first, close enough for me to feel her body heat. My mind churned, fantasies of being with her in other settings brimmed over. *Stop it* I yelled in my mind.

Only one thing to do – start talking, about anything. "Do you think Roniece can work out if she comes back to work for you?" I couldn't have asked a dumber question, but it served my purposes at the moment.

"I hope so. She needs a chance."

We'd decided to walk down the stairs and soon we were at the main door. Juanita stopped first and turned to me, holding out her hand. I grabbed it eagerly and shook it. Her hand was warm and creamy smooth. She gently placed her other hand on the back of mine. My heart hammered away again. Damn it, I was supposed to have all this self-control. I felt a fool. I had to stop myself from leaning in to kiss her.

She smiled widely, invitingly. "I'll call you one way or the other about Marilyn's office." She let go of my hand. "And thanks for your concern about everything. You've helped me feel a great deal better."

"Sure," I said in a dry, barely audible voice.

She turned to walk away. I looked after her, admiring her perfect shape, her simple-yet-classy way of dressing. I left the building, stepping into the delicious sunlight that had burned through an earlier cloud cover. I hoped a breeze wouldn't drift past and knock me over.

Later, I met L.C. downtown at the best steak house in town, Antonio's Restaurant on Juneau Avenue, next to the Milwaukee River. About half as wide as the famous Chicago River, the Milwaukee was lined on both sides with business and apartment buildings built long ago. Quaint old steel and concrete bridges stretched over the river every few hundred yards, as though they were stitching together the two halves of the city.

A light breeze softened the sunny, early evening's warmth, and we ate outside on the patio next to the river. A small motorboat puttered by, creating a spreading wake that lopped lazily against the river's concrete embankments. L.C. chattered happily, and I listened with a token ear. My mind kept drifting back to Juanita, but I somehow managed to hear everything L.C. had to say.

"I'm hoping Roniece's bad little trip's over," L.C. said.

"Me, too." I didn't express my reservations. "Juanita said she'd bring her back to work if she calls."

"Roniece seems to have settled down. She said she'd call Juanita tomorrow. Juanita sounds like fine woman."

"Great. I like happy endings. What is this, the third time it's ended? Feels like Christmas in Hollywood."

L.C. laughed. "Don't be takin' away my snowy Christmases."

When we finished our steak dinners, I got around to mentioning my meeting with Juanita at City Hall and my run-in with Vincent Dragos.

"Cops are pricks," he said. "You know that."

"Some are. A lot aren't."

I then told him about my latest meeting with Four Dead at the penitentiary.

Puffing on a large cigar, L.C. listened with interest.

"At first I thought it was fifty-fifty he'd been there when Earl Jones and the rest got shot," I said. "I'm cautious that way. But after everything, I believe it's as close as possible to one-hundred percent that Four Dead was at those first shootings."

"Shit. It's two-hundred percent."

"I'd agree. But I can't prove it, he won't admit it, and what would it prove if he ever does admit he was there? He likely couldn't – or wouldn't – identify anyone, and there's no known evidence connecting the shooter to the crime. It certainly doesn't make Four Dead – sorry, Reggie – the shooter, or he'd have been tagged for it right away. And there's still no way of knowing how Roniece fits in."

"So, what's your interest?"

"A hunch. An intuition. I feel loose threads between Four Dead and the shooting and Roniece's running from the festival grounds and City Hall, and maybe even Marilyn Chase's murder. How ya' like that?"

L.C.'s smile broadened more and more while I talked. "You crazy."

"I know. But in talking with Juanita Velez and feeling the atmosphere at City Hall, I can't get it out of my head."

L.C. laughed heartily. "I know what you can't get out of your head, and which head you're thinkin' with. I heard that Juanita's a knockout. Everybody lusts after her."

I felt my face flush with both embarrassment and irritation.

"How would you know?"

"I know people, brother." He grinned broadly. "I made some calls."

"I'm not that shallow, L.C. If I wanted to hit on Juanita, I would, without pretenses. . . ."

"I know that too. I'm just yankin' your tail."

My face remained prickly, but I managed to smile. I was blustering – I'd never have the courage to simply "hit" on Juanita Velez.

"Anyway," I said, "I want to see if I can find any evidence, to satisfy my own curiosity. I'm a detective, after all. That's what I do."

L.C. turned his head slightly toward me, narrowing his eyes, keeping his devilish smile. "What is that, exactly?"

"I detect stuff. Okay?"

He held his hands up. "Anything you say, brutha'. I didn't mean you used your detecting game as an angle to get women."

It was good to see L.C. in high spirits. It felt good to have him tease me again.

He brought his hands down and leaned over the table. "Bet you wish Juanita was here, instead of me. Right?"

"Knock it off."

We both laughed.

"Did I mention that Four Dead said the shooter in the Jones killing looked like a ninja dude?" I asked.

"Uh-huh. That's bullshit."

"How so?"

"The brothers don't wear ninja suits to do a killin,' or anything else. They wear ski masks, if anything. Reggie talkin' crazy."

"Maybe it wasn't a brother."

"Who, then? Some 'Mafia man'? I don't think so." He jabbed his cigar toward me. "And you don't, either."

He was most certainly correct. But I'd keep every detail in play while I did my digging. Anyone could have been supplying Jones with his dope – and we were still at the point where anyone could have killed him.

CHAPTER TWELVE

The following day I went again to the Open Records Division of the police department, this time for any and all records or reports on Reginald Thackery. My next stop would be the Clerk of Circuit Court for Reggie's shooting conviction. Since the case was adjudicated, I'd be able to get the complete report and the trial transcript. On my way into the police building, I noticed several vans with TV station logos and satellite dishes parked in front.

News conference. Marilyn Chase. What else would it be?

After entering the building, I looked down the ground-floor hall toward the conference room. A small gathering of people stood outside, looking in through Plexiglas windows. I remembered that Chief Rhodes liked to use the large room for his press conferences. Suspecting he was giving such a conference, I detoured that way to join the group.

When I arrived, Chief Rhodes, in full dress uniform, walked away from the podium while Klieg lights were being shut down. He mingled with some reporters while they stood among the wires and microphones and TV cameras. I hadn't seen him in person in years, but he looked nearly the same. Disappointed at not hearing him speak, I turned away.

I went to the third floor for Reggie's records, which I was told would take a while to prepare. I decided to go back down to the ground-floor snack area to wait. When I reached the bottom floor the elevator doors opened, and Chief Rhodes stood in the hall about 20 feet away. Several high-ranking officers were with him. He looked in my direction and did a minor double take.

"Hey, Jack," he said, waving his arm. "How are you?"

The brass with him turned toward me with empty expressions on their faces. None of them knew me from my days with the department. Rookies. All rookies. He stepped away from them and walked briskly toward me. I was surprised and speechless, but felt honored at being singled out. We'd been good friends, but had drifted apart after his promotions and my leaving the force.

"Jack Blanchard, my man," he said while grabbing my hand and pumping it with both of his.

He looked genuinely pleased to see me. His command staff remained behind, appearing perplexed.

"Hi, Chief," I said, feeling uneasy. Heavy brass always did that to me. "How's it going?"

"I miss you, Jack. I miss the old days, I really do."

"That bad, huh?"

He rolled his eyes and smiled slightly, but remained otherwise inscrutable. "There's a lot going on these days." He made a knowing expression. "Lots o' pressure."

"The big bucks always bring that sort of thing."

"Oh, don't give me that." He smiled playfully, seemingly ready for a round of ribbing. Just like the old days, when we were partners. He started to laugh. "Even if you're right, don't give me that."

He motioned me toward the elevator. "Gotta keep moving, the reporters are still around."

We walked together slowly. His staff moved forward at the same pace we did, but kept their distance, apparently sensing that he wanted to speak privately with me.

"That City Hall thing's got to be a mess," I said, knowing I wouldn't get a straight response.

He stopped and made a feigned expression of pain. "I'd love to be able to talk about it, about the whole thing – investigative angles, politics, back rooms filled with smoke and mirrors and idiots."

We both smiled and suppressed our laughter. I noticed that his entourage had also stopped. They quietly stared at us.

"You know the score," he said. "It's the kind of stuff we'd have chewed over endlessly when we were partners."

I couldn't help myself. "Any clues? Any leads?"

He laughed, shook his head, and looked me in the eyes. "That's my answer. The train ain't ready to leave the station." He brought a hand up to cup his mouth and said in an exaggerated whisper, "That's what I just got done telling the news media. They think the police and D.A.'s office are holding out, but that's not so."

I didn't believe him for a minute – his favorite pastime was playing button-button with the press. His Homicide Squad was nipping at Mayor McCord's heels even as we spoke. Had to be. I knew him too well. But I was flattered. Having a police chief be so openly cordial with someone like me, even though I'd been a friend, was completely unexpected. Yet, I was suspicious. I sensed an ulterior motive.

I knew him too well.

"I gotta run," he said, sticking his hand out to shake mine again. "It was good to see you, Jack. You look great, and I've heard you're doing great business, especially since your big case with that guy. What was his name?"

"L.C. Veasley. That was years ago."

"That was a good catch. Everybody thought so." He waved and turned toward the elevator, which had just arrived. He jauntily stepped into the car, with his forlorn gang of commanding officers following him like ducklings after their mother. They were chasing one of a kind. They'd never catch up.

The strange incident with the chief had snagged in my thoughts while I returned to the Open Records Division. If I'd run into the chief while he was off duty, I would have understood his being so personal. Something was going on, but I decided to tuck it away for the time being.

After picking up Reggie's records, which clearly detailed his life as a common criminal, I went to the Clerk of Courts office next to the police building for the file of his murder conviction. After copying the reports, I sat in the lobby and read them over. I could see why the cops and the D.A. didn't believe Reggie's story about a robbery attempt and self-defense.

Two eyewitnesses to the shooting said they'd seen Reggie and his attackers hanging around together all the time before the day of the incident. The witnesses were probably involved with drugs themselves, and I had the feeling that they'd also known about Earl Jones's drug dealing and murder two weeks before. But nothing about that had been brought up during their testimony, and they'd come off looking like objective third parties. Four Dead was dead meat from the get-go.

The D.A. had no problem selling the case to the jury as a drug war shootout. Several other witnesses said they'd seen Reggie fire the first shots. That may or may not have been true, but the D.A. got his conviction, and Reggie got a 10-year rocket ride.

The extensive criminal records of the two dead men – Antjuan Borders and Jamal McKee – including complete sets of police investigations of their crimes committed before their murders, were included in the file. I pored over the material. You never know when or how names, places, and dates can connect dots that trace a clearer picture, but my heart wasn't in it. The odds against it were too extreme. But I hung in, hoping to find something that was at least interesting.

Disheartened, I came to the last page – an arrest report for Jamal McKee on a narcotics violation four years earlier. He'd been convicted, but was given probation. How the hell could that be, with his criminal record? Even the most lenient judge wouldn't have done that without a damn good reason.

I smelled a deal, one that ordinarily wouldn't have been made with someone who had the habitual criminality of McKee. He must have been more than just a snitch who worked off his time by setting up drug busts. It must have been super big-time stuff for him not to go to jail. I smelled a bad deal, one that allowed McKee, an inveterate drug dealer, to return to the streets and continue his trade.

Juanita Velez had mentioned that Vince Dragos was a narcotics dick at one time. I wondered if Dragos knew anything about McKee. I wondered who could ask him and get a straight answer. I knew it wouldn't be me, and I decided to forget about it.

I'd actually connected some dots – Reggie and Earl Jones to Antjuan Borders and Jamal McKee – however unclear was its meaning. But I felt a little excitement, just chasing an intriguing criminal trail. I hadn't done that since . . . well, since I worked on

L.C. Veasley's case. The prospect of digging deeper had me tripping.

There was one problem. In order to find anything truly important, I'd need inside information from the police. As the old saying goes, I had a better chance of being hit by lightning. But there are ways of getting yourself hit – find a lightning rod and grab it during a thunderstorm. Good plan. I gathered my notes and left.

Later that afternoon I listened to a news broadcast on my car radio. . . .

"Today," the male announcer began, "Mayor McCord communicated through a spokesperson that he'd been interviewed by police detectives regarding Marilyn Chase's murder. He added that he'd give a statement to the media within a few days.

"This on the heels of Police Chief Jerome Rhodes's morning press conference where he stated that his department was continuing its investigation and that he had nothing to report at this time."

The city's two top officials had said a lot of nothing, but one could easily read between the lines. The police hadn't yet ruled out the mayor as a suspect, and the mayor was sweating. Even if I were innocent, I wouldn't want to have been in the mayor's shoes. The situation had everything the news media loved – sex, murder, and intrigue – all in the highest places. If the mayor didn't do it, the cops had better find who did, or the erupting scandal would forever mark him.

CHAPTER THIRTEEN

It would be a daunting challenge to get classified, or certain "protected" information, from the cops. Daunting, not impossible, because I'd done it few times in the past, albeit regarding minor incidents. But at that moment I couldn't think about it. I was busy thinking about Juanita. I wanted to hear her voice more than to investigate anything.

But more than that, I needed to go over the police reports and notes I'd obtained, and I'd have to force myself to focus. Having my ducks lined up would be important when I gave my pitch to some cop at the police department. I planned on staying home the rest of the day, give myself a treat with a bottle or two of Guinness, go to bed happy, and start fresh in the morning.

At six o'clock that evening a call came in on my private cell phone line while I sat at my kitchen table staring blankly at all the paperwork. It had all run together, with me finding nothing more than I'd already noted.

"Are you busy?" a timid, kitten-soft woman's voice asked when I answered.

I wasn't sure who it was. "Juanita?" I asked. "Is that you?"

"Yes, Jack. It's me."

She sounded different than the other times I'd spoken with her – less stressed, more personal. I envisioned her being at home rather than her office. I stood and walked to the living room, switched off the TV, and sat in the lounge chair. I was glad I hadn't started drinking

Guinness yet.

"Are you still at work?" I asked.

"No. I got home a little while ago."

My instincts were better than my self-control. I felt tongue-tied, nervous. "So, ah . . . so, what's up?" I asked, managing to subdue a tremolo in my voice.

"I went through Marilyn's office. The police had left it a little messy after their search. Being in there shook me up."

"Did they ransack the place?"

"Not seriously. They left some desk and file drawers open, some papers lying around. They also took Marilyn's computer monitor. I don't know why they did that. She worked off the network hard drive, like we all do. The monitor contains no information. I guess the police experts aren't quite so expert. And I got spooked – Marilyn's dead, and here I am rummaging around in her personal things."

I began to relax. "I understand."

"Anyway, it appeared that the only thing they'd taken was the monitor."

Seizing the monitor made some sense to me. Homicide detectives, not computer experts, would have done the basic room search and taken certain "gross" items, such as the computer monitor. They'd take it just to be safe, and let the specialists do their thing later.

"Someone thinks they're gonna get some goodies," I said. "They'll be disappointed when they learn they need her hard drive entries."

"So, we haven't gained anything."

"Looks like it. But anything we learn can be important. At least we know the cops are looking in a certain direction. But I'd hoped there'd have been something obvious to you that wasn't to the cops."

She breathed heavily into the phone. Finally, she asked, "Do you actually think it's possible that Marilyn found out something and was killed because of it?"

"I can't think of another reason, other than the mayor killed her over a love spat. Maybe something about Marilyn leaving for state government. . . ."

"That wasn't it. The mayor helped her get that post. She'd have been here as often as the State Capitol."

"That answers that. Marilyn did say a scandal was lurking that would rock City Hall." A thought occurred to me. "Does Roniece know other people who work at City Hall? Could she have seen someone she knows from there at the festival grounds, and she ran because she was afraid? You know, there could be some kind of old link because of Councilman Artic and his daughter."

"I'd hate to think that. I don't personally suspect anyone, but I believe Marilyn had started checking things out."

"Maybe Roniece had only been freaked out. It's just a hunch."

Juanita laughed, more of a purring sound. "There's no such thing as a *bad* hunch."

"Right." I felt my smile growing so wide it threatened to split my cheeks. "I think we should stay in touch for a while. I'll talk to you tomorrow."

"Good. I'll be looking forward to your call."

After hanging up, I went to the refrigerator and opened a bottle of Guinness. I decided to finish re-reading the police reports later. Returning to the living room, I sat back in my easy chair and stared off blankly, slowly sipping the dark Irish brew. The day had been one for the books, and I wanted to savor it along with my refreshment.

The following morning I got up early and finished reading the police reports. I decided my only way of getting inside dope from the cops was to start off using my own information about Four Dead – I'd continued thinking of Reggie as "Four Dead," it made me feel more down and dirty – and see if I could weasel my way from there. I organized some notes and prepared to call. I stopped, instead pouring a cup of coffee. I wasn't worried about catching some sassy talk from a wise-assed cop. I *was* worried about hitting a stone wall.

I quickly went through my notes again, finished my coffee, and finally called the police department's Detective Bureau. A clerk transferred me to the records section, and a female police officer answered the phone. After introducing myself, I started by telling her about Reginald Thackery, mentioned his new nickname of "Four Dead" and his murder conviction, and that I might have some important information about him. I'd also made sure to mention I was a former city police detective, former partner of Chief Rhodes. Small stuff like that.

"Oh, really?" she said. "When did you work here?"

"A few years ago. More than 10."

"Whoa, that's way before my time." She did not seem impressed. "Normally, you'd need to come in person. But I'll see if you check out."

We both hung up and she called me back a few minutes later.

"Some of the old goats groaned when I mentioned your name, but I got the okay to do phone work. . . . Let's see. Reginald Thackery. Now calls himself 'Four Dead,' since he went to the joint a year-and-a-half ago. 'Four Dead.' Interesting alias."

She should have only known.

She breathed harshly into the phone while shuffling through some paperwork. "I checked Mr. Thackery out and he's got a file. I was told to patch you over to Detective Will Tandy, who'll discuss things with you."

"Yeah, Detective Tandy," the officer answered in a forceful, gravely voice after he picked up my call.

I understood his type immediately – competent, confident, and impossible to scam. I introduced myself and re-explained some of what I'd told the first officer.

He cut me off sharply. "I know your story. We've also gotten some calls along the way from other prison inmates about Reginald Thackery, or 'Four Dead,' as you've found out. Used to be they call themselves new religious names – 'Muhammad,' 'Abdullah,' and stuff. The callers all wanted to remain anonymous, unless we made a case. Of course, they want to be set free in exchange for their information."

"I'm very sure you'll do just that."

He laughed.

I moved right along. "I've talked to this Four Dead character twice, and both times he sounded as though he'd been some kind of witness to a quadruple drug murder in an alley a couple years ago."

"Earl Jones, Kim Artic, Tray Clincy, and Malcolm Downes."

"Right. . . ."

"I investigated it," he said impatiently.

This was gonna take a load of primo country bullshit, the kind you get before it hits the ground. "Good. I can get right to the point."

"The point is," Detective Tandy said, notching up the volume of his gravelly voice, "I took the first call on this Thackery – or 'Four Dead' character – and tried to set up an interview with him at the prison, but he doesn't want to talk to the po-lice, so I never went to see him."

At least Tandy was talking to me. And he was being polite. I told him how Four Dead had chosen his nickname, and the images of the shooting he claimed to have in his head. I didn't mention that he was a diagnosed schizophrenic.

He listened at first without comment, and then said, "The prison snitches told us all that. Word is one of his fellow inmates started calling him 'Four D,' a shortened version of his nickname, because he came up short with his story. I guess it started a fight."

"I can imagine." A jailhouse thing, just the way I'd figured.

"Some thought he might have done it, but there's no evidence or witnesses to that effect. And, there's a note in here that he's a diagnosed schizophrenic. Wouldn't he be a wonderful witness?"

Everybody knew everything before me. I should've guessed.

"I know, he'd be terrible," I said. "But he's so detailed and consistent with his story, it makes you wonder. Doesn't it?"

"No. Some schizos can be that way. You know, seemingly under control, especially if they've been taking their meds with some regularity."

Tandy's ready knowledge of everything I'd gotten was further evidence that he was on the ball.

He said, "We've been coming across more and more schizophrenics since crack cocaine became widespread. Schizos instantly become heavily addicted to crack and go on wild-assed crime sprees to support their habit. Crack's the worst thing we've seen."

I was growing depressed. "That's what I've heard."

Tandy continued. "But, anything's possible. So I checked Thackery out six ways to Sunday, found a couple minor links between him and people we know were involved with Jones and the rest, but there was nothing else to go on."

Tandy was willing to talk, but was completely impersonal. I

plowed ahead. "Four Dead's locked up for killing two dope runners in a shootout who were associated with Earl Jones. Happened two weeks after—"

"I know all about it, that's part of what I checked on."

He'd become short with me, sounding ready to hang up. I started getting desperate. "Those victims were real scum. Bad drug records. One of them was never sentenced on his last drug bust, despite a horrible record. Must've snitched his way out of it."

I hoped that sounding like an insider would give me some leverage. It's a technique that can work with the unsuspecting, but Detective Tandy was the type who suspected everything.

"That information wouldn't be in these reports, and narcs protect their informant's identities better than the Secret Service protects the President."

I hoped he might refer me to the Narcotics Squad. I should have known better. "Looks like it could be a daisy chain, the four killed in the alley, then Four Dead's shootout with Jones's runners."

"We've known all along that it's interconnected, but we can't prove anything. Having been a cop, you know how it is. Nobody says nothin'."

"Yeah, I remember – long time ago that it was."

"I checked you out with my boss, Lieutenant DuPont," he said, a cynical tone in his voice. "Says he was still in uniform when you and Chief Rhodes were partners in the Detective Bureau. He said you guys had great reputations."

This was actually the first time I'd tried using whatever influence I might still have since I left the department – my business being mostly helping defense attorneys with appeals, checking alibis of the accused, and civil matters. It felt strange. Tandy was too forthcoming about it.

I didn't want to show my surprise. "And the only possibility you guys have regarding the murders is a squirrel in a cage," I said without acknowledging his allusion to my reputation.

"I didn't say that. There's things in the investigation that no one knows but us. I said the 'squirrel in a cage' is useless to us at this time. Being mostly crazy, this Four Dead character would have to lead us to other people or evidence, and how can anyone hope that would happen? Like I said, he won't even let us visit his cage."

He must have felt the way I did when I was a cop. Maybe someday he'd become overly cynical and bug out, the way I had.

Nah . . . he sounded like a lifer.

"You say you've talked to him twice?" Tandy asked.

I laughed. "Yeah. I think he likes me."

He remained silent.

"What?" I asked. "What about it?"

"Nothing. I, ah, I'm glad you've established a good rapport."

"Yeah, it helps get information." I stopped short. One mustn't talk smart to the police, especially a cop who's cooperating with you.

"Thanks for the tip," Tandy said, ready to ring me off.

"Yeah, sure. I'm still working on some things, and I'll call you if I get anything more."

"You're working on what, exactly?"

I was caught without a ready answer. As with Detective Dragos, he wouldn't like it if he thought I was working on a police investigation.

"Well, Four Dead was brought to my attention by people who know him, and they might have more to say." I couldn't have sounded less convincing, but I wasn't about to tell Tandy of my real activities – like at City Hall, for instance.

"Sounds okay to me. You know your boundaries. If you ever get anything good, I'll make sure you get proper recognition," he said with a laugh. "I'm sorry, but I won't hold my breath."

"Neither will I."

We both hung up. Nothing. He'd given me nothing, because he had nothing, not just because I was an outsider. I felt ridiculous after all, wondering just what the hell I'd expected get.

I thought about his interest in my relationship with Four Dead, which seemed odd. I'd keep that in mind.

My fax machine hummed and started spitting paper. I checked – it was L.C. letting me know he'd transferred funds for my work on Roniece's case to my bank. Case closed. Nice. The god of timing taking its cue now to let me know that I was finished. But my effort to sink into deep, suffocating despair failed. I'd met Juanita Velez, whose unexpected appearance in my life had added colors and vibrations I hadn't felt in a long while. Even if thoughts of her were only foolish fancy, and most certainly they were – it eased the pain of my failure. I laughed. My skeptical mind instantly reached for the assurance that once Juanita poofed out of my life, I'd be hit with a sense of double-barreled failure.

It looked like another Guinness night, maybe with some Old Bushmills Irish whisky for a chaser. I'd have to stop at the liquor store to make that happen. I couldn't think that far ahead.

Later that day, more news came over the TV and radio stations about Mayor McCord, that he'd been told to report to the D.A.'s office with his attorney regarding the Marilyn Chase murder. The reaction was certain to be as though a tidal wave had broken over the lakefront and smashed through the city. The principals involved were being tight-lipped as to why the D.A. called the mayor in, which one naïve radio newscaster seemed not to understand.

Naïve news reporters should be put on a slow boat.

I stopped. The suffocating depths were still there, waiting for me to think my way into them, and this was one of countless ruminations that could do the trick.

The whole city would be wondering what evidence there was against the mayor. They wouldn't be informed until the D.A. and cops were ready. Why didn't everyone accept that? I knew why they couldn't, but the answer was too dreary to recount.

I didn't buy any Old Bushmills and I didn't drink any Guinness that night. They would have taken me to bad places in my head, and I decided to wait awhile before I got depressed.

CHAPTER FOURTEEN

The next two days brought the depression I'd expected. Juanita didn't call. I didn't want to be a pest, so I left it alone. More news broke about Mayor McCord. Apparently some evidence of an undisclosed type linking him to Marilyn Chase's murder had been found in his car, and the car was impounded. It seemed as though the D.A. was ready to charge him with her killing. I don't know why hearing that depressed me, except maybe that I'd have no excuse to call Juanita again if that were the case. I'd have to call for personal reasons, and that scared me.

I know. A woman will tell you, all you have to do is ask. I'm good at detecting, not asking.

I had enough to do . . . cleaning up a ton of correspondence that had been waiting, faxing records and reports to – whom else? – defense attorneys. My relationship with them had worked out strangely – from me trying as a cop to put their clients in jail, to me trying as a PI to get them out of jail. It didn't bother me, PIs rarely succeed at it, and the attorneys are realistic – they know their clients are guilty, and don't expect more than some background information that can possibly mitigate their clients' sentences.

Unusual it is when an attorney has good reason to believe that a client is innocent. I'd actually cleared people in minor cases of that type – disorderly conducts, traffic cases, and some thefts where witnesses recanted their identification of the defendants.

There was one major exception I was involved with that made

newspaper headlines, but I never expected it to happen again.

I spent the day alone, avoiding making or receiving personal phone calls, and places where I'd likely run into people I knew. It seemed that my agreement with Juanita to keep in touch no matter what had gone by the wayside. I was tempted to call her more than once, but felt like a phony – my motivation was purely personal. I'd had bad experiences trying to finagle get-togethers with women based on pretenses of pursuing an investigation. Juanita's feelings were too important. I'd decided to be patient.

But I'd also remained anxious and depressed, going through my unrequited, juvenile love jones.

Juanita finally did call on my cell phone the afternoon of the second day, and upon hearing her voice my dark horizons momentarily became dotted with cheery lights and party balloons. Unfortunately, the conversation was anything but pleasant.

"It's awful, what's happening to Mayor McCord," she'd led off saying, her voice cracking.

"They found evidence in his car."

"What evidence? No one at City Hall knows."

"I know, they haven't said. But it must be good for the D.A. to push this hard, and to go public."

"No one here believes Arthur McCord murdered Marilyn Chase, goddamn it. Least of all me."

I was shocked not so much by her cursing but the anger and intensity in her voice. "I know, kiddo. We've been over this." I overlooked her pique. "We'll just have to wait and see."

A long, awkward pause followed, after which I said, "Juanita?"

She breathed out heavily. "I want to go to Marilyn's house."

Another shock. "And do what?"

"Look around. See if anything's there."

"You're kidding." She was looking for trouble, and she'd find it quickly by trespassing Marilyn's house.

"I wouldn't trespass. I know her sister Julia quite well. I'm sure that if I explained myself, she'd let me in to look around."

"It's standard procedure for the police to immediately search houses of homicide victims. What would you hope to find that they didn't?"

"I don't know. Anything. Something the police wouldn't think is important. That's why I want you to come with me."

The shocks kept coming. "You're becoming obsessed, Juanita. I hate to say it, but I think our little investigation is over."

"Will you go with me?" She wasn't about to take "no" for an answer.

I thought for a moment. "If you get permission and a key, I don't see what it could hurt."

"Good. I'd like to do it tonight."

She'd showed an aggressiveness I hadn't suspected. But I'd only go along with so much before I pulled the plug. Amateur sleuths tend to quickly get out of control.

"Tonight is fine. What time?"

"I work late, but I'll eat on the run afterward. Say, eight o'clock?"

"Want me to pick you up?"

"That would be great. I didn't mean to be presumptuous."

"No problem. By the way, I'm screening my calls for the rest of the day, so if you have to, call my home number. I'll pick up when I know it's you."

She gave me her address and home phone number and we hung up. I shut off my cell phone – I didn't want any piss calls interrupting my plans with Juanita. She sounded close to the edge, but I figured I could handle her. Talking to Marilyn's sister first was a must. Her sister could even come along. I had no hope that we'd find anything meaningful. In fact, I knew we wouldn't. But I went along with it to indulge Juanita – let her find closure – and, of course, to have a chance to be with her.

Eight o'clock couldn't come soon enough. At 7:40 I went to pick her up. The half-light of early evening loomed when I arrived at her house, which was tucked behind trees and shrubs, in a quiet, well-to-do neighborhood. The front sidewalk was short and curved, leading through narrow path of tall evergreen trees. The small but posh-looking house was made of heavy, cream-colored stone. Its steeply pitched roof was covered with overlapping cedar shingles. The place looked clean and classy.

I rang the doorbell and Juanita invited me in. She'd obviously freshened herself, wore a lightly scented perfume that smelled heavenly, and smiled when I entered her home.

She stepped forward to embrace me in a friendly way. I fought the temptation to hold her tight.

"Have you called Marilyn's sister?" I asked.

"I've been trying, but there's no answer."

She stepped back and put her hand on my arm. "I hope I'm not imposing."

Impose. Impose away. "If I couldn't have come, I wouldn't have."

She was all business. "I'd like to drive past Marilyn's house first. I'll keep calling her sister on my cell phone."

We left immediately. Juanita directed me while I drove. In a short while we arrived at Marilyn's house. The place, a two-story Cape Cod, was completely dark. We sat in my car in front, the engine running, neither of us saying anything. Juanita remained motionless while staring at the house. She removed her cell phone from her purse and pushed the redial button. "Her sister's still not answering." After a few moments she said, "Could we drive around to the back? There's an alley in this block."

As long as we stayed in the car I felt all right. If she wanted to get out and prowl around before contacting her sister, I'd have to put on the brakes. I drove slowly through the alley with my headlights on. No one was around. All the neighboring homes had their lights on. It was a quiet, safe neighborhood. Juanita pushed the redial button on her phone again, but I had the sinking feeling that there'd be no answer before Juanita started pushing to go in.

We stopped in the alley at the rear of Marilyn's house. Despite the darkness we were able to see the back yard and backside of the building. I turned off the car's headlights but let the engine idle.

"Do you have a flashlight?" Juanita asked.

"Why?"

She sighed. "No reason."

I smiled. Reaching over my seat to the floor in back, I said, "Sure. What's a PI without a flashlight?"

A moment later she said, "I want to go closer."

"You mean walk up to the house, right? Why? Can't you wait 'til you talk to Marilyn's sister?"

She leaned toward me. "There'll be no problem. Marilyn and I were very close. I've been here a lot. The neighbors know me."

I turned to look again at the back of the house. She leaned more heavily against me.

"Let's just walk around," she said. "I'll keep calling Marilyn's sister."

Her soft breasts pressed against me while she leaned on my arm and chest. I turned my head back to look at her. Her face was an inch from mine. A waft of her perfume came even closer – touching my skin, drifting into my nose. Her long, luxurious hair swept across my cheek when she moved. Straining to look more closely at the house, she leaned even harder against me. I didn't complain.

"The neighbors won't recognize you in the dark," I said. "You and I will just be shadowy figures skulking around, and they'll call the cops."

She leaned away. Deep furrows built on her brow and a tear slipped down her cheek. She smudged the tear away with the palm of her hand.

"I feel foolish," she said. "Embarrassed and foolish."

"It's all right. I know how it feels to be driven."

"I've got to know what happened to my friend." She began to cry and hugged me tight around the neck. "I *am* driven. Obsessed. I've got to know what Marilyn was on to."

A he-man hubris swelled within. It felt as though Tarzan was beating my chest, but it was only my thumping heart. I put the car in park and turned off the engine.

"I'll get out and check around," I said. "You wait here, just in case. Keep calling Marilyn's sister."

It was against my better judgment, but I thought, what could happen? I'd simply be embarrassed if a neighbor saw me and called the police. Odds were pretty good that Juanita could explain it away. I probably wouldn't go to jail. My detective license wouldn't necessarily be at risk.

"You and Marilyn were *really* close, right?" I asked. "I mean the neighbors and her sister would vouch for you, and everything."

"Oh, yes. I've no doubt."

Adrenaline began pumping through me while I prepared to get out of the car. A voice of reason shouted in my head to forget it, to wait or drive off. But I wanted to please Juanita. She was so sincere, so charmingly naïve, I couldn't bear disappointing her. Reason be damned. I grabbed my high beam lantern, and opened the car door.

"Make sure you stay here," I reminded her.

I stayed on the lawn while approaching the back door, the unlit lantern in my hand, swinging at my side. The back yard was dark beneath a starless, moonless sky. I arrived at a three-step cement porch, walked up and stood at the door. I reached for the door handle and found it dented and broken, usually the sign of a forced entry. I couldn't imagine that the cops hadn't used a key to get in when they searched. I pushed on the door. It easily swung inward.

I flashed the light into the hallway and some rooms beyond. The place was badly ransacked. Someone had been there besides the cops.

Stepping back and down the steps to size up the situation, I bumped hard into another person.

"Ow!" a woman's voice said. It was Juanita. She fell off the steps and onto the ground.

I'd staggered off the porch and fallen also. "You scared the hell out of me," I said in a hoarse whisper while getting to my feet and helping her up. "I thought I told you to stay in the car."

She brushed herself off and rubbed her backside with both hands. "I got scared, being all alone. I'd rather get in trouble with you here than by myself in the car."

I should have thought of that. But then if I had, I'd have never left the car. It was too late now. I took her hand and held it tight. "Someone broke in. I'm afraid we're going to have to stop here, and call the police."

Though I strongly doubted it, someone could still have been inside. In one sense, it wasn't much of a coincidence, Marilyn's house being burglarized after she was killed. A fairly common method of operation is for creeps to see a death notice in the newspaper and break into the dead person's house on the day of the funeral. I shook my head. That wasn't it.

While still standing next to the porch, Juanita pressed her body hard against my back. She trembled. I heard her breath coming in short bursts, felt it blow on my neck. But I was too juiced to feel the tingles I'd have ordinarily felt. No movement or sound came from inside the house. The neighboring houses were quiet. The night was balmy and still.

"We gotta go back to the car," I said, still gripping her clammy hand, which felt like dead flesh.

"Is someone still inside?" she asked.

"I don't know. That's the cops' job to find out."

I led her back to my car and we both got in, quietly closing our doors. Juanita called the police on her cell phone and told them we'd stand by until they came. Then she called Marilyn's sister again, who still didn't answer.

The responding uniformed police officers met us at my car in the alley. We gave them brief statements. A tall, blonde female officer asked, "What were you doing back here?"

Juanita explained who she was – her position at City Hall, and her relationship to Marilyn Chase. The officer listened without expression while Juanita described her grief-driven need to drive past Marilyn's house.

"Humph," the officer said when I showed her my PI license.

Meanwhile, her male partner trotted through the back yard toward the front of the house. Before following him, she said, "You two stay here."

We remained in my car while the officers checked all sides of the house, and then entered to search. Through the house windows I occasionally saw flashlight beams quickly flare on and off, as though they were silent muzzle flashes of discharging firearms. One by one, the house lights went on, until the entire place was lit.

In a short while the female officer returned to my car. She leaned down, and through my open window said, "It's a burglary. I wonder why a neighbor didn't see an open back door." She held my gaze while she spoke.

"Well, we walked around a bit," I said sheepishly. "The back door was closed, but when I looked close I saw the dent in the door handle."

"Wait until we're done with the preliminaries," she said. "We're gonna check the neighbors and see what they say." She straightened and called on her portable radio for a mobile evidence technician to meet her.

I looked at Juanita with raised eyebrows. "A burglary," I said in a low voice.

"I don't know what to think."

CHAPTER FIFTEEN

The police released us and I drove back to Juanita's house. We barely spoke. I sensed her embarrassment at insisting on going to Marilyn's home. At least we'd discovered that a crime had been committed, and notified the authorities. The possibility occurred to me that the burglary might not have been committed by some random drug addict.

"Want to come in?" Juanita said after we arrived at her house and walked to the front door.

I accepted her invitation. Inside, Juanita directed me to her living room to sit on a soft black leather chair. She sat on my left, on an earth-toned cloth sofa.

After settling in her seat, she sighed and said, "What do you think?"

"I'm thinking the burglary may have been done by someone other than the typical sneak thief."

She looked away from me and pursed her lips. "Why do you think that?"

"Because I don't believe in coincidences."

"So you've said." She placed a palm to her forehead and said, "What am I thinking? Would you like a drink? I certainly could use something."

I flinched inwardly. I'd never had a drink at the home of a client. Even though Juanita hadn't hired me, it felt as though she had. But then – what the hell? There were no laws against drinking with clients

– it was only my personal rule. And again, damn it, Juanita wasn't a client. I felt both excited and guilty.

She was looking at me expectantly.

"Sure," I said.

"I don't have much of a choice," she said while getting up and going to her kitchen. "I'm not a drinker."

"Do you have wine?" I asked, figuring that everyone has wine on hand. Come to think of it, I didn't. But, then . . .

She appeared in the kitchen doorway, across the room from where I sat. She leaned against the doorframe, smiling strangely, blushing slightly.

"I have a nice German Riesling," she said. "In the back of my 'fridge. It's white and sweet. It's been there forever. I usually limit wine drinking to dinnertime. When I have people over, of course."

"I like a sweet white wine." I actually preferred something dry and red.

Still smiling, she returned to the kitchen and came back with an unopened wine bottle, and two glasses. She returned to the sofa, placed the glasses on a glass-top coffee table before us, and handed me the unopened bottle. "Would you please?"

After twisting off the cap and pouring each glass half full, I returned the bottle to the coffee table.

We toasted silently and sipped our wine. She looked straight ahead, at first with a puzzled look. She arched her brow, flattened her lips in apparent frustration, then relaxed and sighed once again. She took a few more quick sips. I was fascinated watching her.

She turned to me, her face pleated by a hard, inquiring look. "So, are you thinking that whoever killed Marilyn also broke into her house?"

She was smart, and got right to the point.

I looked directly at her. "It's plausible, yeah, but right now there's only coincidence."

"The coincidence you don't believe in."

"Right."

"And, assuming you're correct, the killer would search Marilyn's house for any evidence that could link him to her murder."

"Or link her."

"Or her. Right." She paused. "Do you think the police can figure it out?"

"If they get evidence. Unfortunately, the odds are against that, in any particular burglary investigation."

"You don't think the mayor . . ."

I shook my head. "I'm with you. No way the mayor did a murder and a chicken shit burglary afterward. First, he'd likely have a key to Marilyn's house and wouldn't have to break in. And he couldn't afford to be seen there.

"And I can't believe he killed Marilyn. For one thing, the murder was too sloppy. Her body was found right away. She was obviously a homicide victim, a crime that most probably happened spontaneously. Without anything else to go on, the police would automatically suspect him, and he'd certainly have known that.

"Then again, he could've broken in to Marilyn's house to make it look like a typical house burglary. If he did, the cops'll figure it out."

She nodded slowly. "Do you think the police have Marilyn's murder figured out?"

"My gut tells me no. I feel the cops and D.A. playing too much cat and mouse with the mayor-as-suspect angle. They've only asked him to come in for an interview, not made an arrest based on the 'evidence' they found in his car. That's important. If they don't have enough to arrest him outright, they're still struggling."

She looked away from me and sat forward on the sofa, her knees squeezed tightly together, her arms clamped in at her sides. She looked bewildered, and frightened and sad, all at once.

"Could Marilyn have put any notes about Roniece and everything on her computer at work?" I asked.

She picked up her wine glass and took a drink. "She'd have used diskettes, or re-writable CDs, not the network hard drive. She didn't trust flash drives not to fail."

"Did she have a computer at home?"

"Yes. A laptop."

"She'd probably use that one to store any information. Right?"

"She wouldn't keep information like that on any hard drive. She was too smart. She'd keep the disks with her, and use them in a computer with compatible software."

"That's true." I hadn't known that. I knew nothing about computers beyond word processing and making record checks on the Internet. I took a sip of my wine, then another before setting the glass back down. Juanita had emptied her glass.

"More?" she said, holding her glass up to me.

"Sure."

I finished the rest of my wine with a gulp, grabbed the bottle from the coffee table, poured both our glasses half full, and set the bottle back down. Juanita grabbed the bottle and filled both our glasses to the rim, then set the bottle on the carpet next to her. She did it in a businesslike manner, as though she were saying, "It's gonna be a long night, pal."

"I'd like to know what the cops found missing in her house," I said.

"Can't you find out from the police report? That's public record. Right?"

"Yes. Normally I can, but it'll take a day. Maybe two. But this one ain't so normal."

"Unless you called someone you knew to help you out. From your days on the force, I mean."

"That's iffy. I don't have a sure 'in' with anyone. I'll probably have to wait for the public report, the way everyone else does." I purposely did not mention my long-ago association with Chief Rhodes. I had no faith that it would get me anywhere after the lengthy passage of time.

She looked at me with surprise. "You don't know anyone, any more? How do you get things done as a PI?" She took a deep swallow of her wine. Her glass was more than half empty.

Hubris leaped through me once again. "I know the chief," I said on impulse, with an exaggerated smile. "He and I were partners as detectives, many moons ago."

She raised her glass toward me. "There you go."

"Sorry, but I haven't kept close ties with him. I can't simply pick up the phone and call. Anyway, the department wouldn't even release the basics if the homicide investigators found something hot."

"Darn," she said, and drank the rest of her wine. "More?"

she asked, while picking up the bottle and pouring herself another glassful.

I held my glass toward her, and she again filled it to the rim. I watched her closely. For the first time since we'd left Marilyn Chase's house I reflected on Juanita's beauty, allowed my affection for her to run free. I fixated on her – a little too long.

"Is everything all right?" She was looking at me with curiosity. Her cheeks were becoming rosy from the wine. Her eyes glistened.

"Oh, yeah. I'm just thinking." Thinking of her, for a moment. And it was a damned wonderful feeling. I felt heat rising to my face . . . from the wine as well as my flight of fancy. Juanita. Juanita. I was losing more control by the moment.

She returned my gaze, then looked down – breaking me from my daydream. An uneasy quiet lingered, but it brought me back to Earth.

She looked at me again, eyes wide, a slight smile pushing at her reddened cheeks. "So, where do you think this is going?" She leaned a little closer and raised her eyebrows.

Wherever you want.

"My investigation?" I said. "It doesn't look too good. Remember, I was hired by L.C. to find Roniece, and she's found. I'm doing this extra stuff strictly on my own – and to help you.

"Roniece's cooperation would help me immensely – in my wildest dreams she'd help me solve some murders – but I'm certain she wouldn't talk to me."

"Maybe I can coax her the next time I speak with her."

"Don't count on it. Whatever went on with her is dark, and probably kinda dirty. She never went to the police, which makes me suspicious."

"Suspicious of what?"

"Her motive for keeping her mouth shut. She's probably afraid of even more repercussions than she's already had."

Juanita set her glass on the table and sat back. "It's unlikely we'll ever know what Marilyn was onto. Right?"

I hesitated. "Unlikely that we will, yes. I have no idea where the police may go with it."

She looked at me. "Are you going to keep trying?"

"I'll play it to the end, although the end seems to be at hand."

She sat forward and grabbed her glass, which she held up in a toast. "Then here's to drinking more wine." She giggled and took a drink.

"Hear, hear." I raised my glass to my lips.

"My cheeks feel hot," she said, turning her face to me. "Are they red?" Her eyes were glassy. A constant grin decorated her face.

"Wine stained, I'd say."

She laughed. "I normally drink wine with food," she said, reiterating her earlier point. "But this is tasting good."

She exuded the shine and good health of one who drinks little, or not at all. It was good to see her relax. I felt relaxed, too.

"How long have you worked at City Hall?" I asked. Good. Smooth segue.

She didn't hesitate. "Four years. As I said, Marilyn got me the job. Until now, I'd been having the most wonderful time of my life."

"Your whole life?"

She raised her glass again. "My who-o-o-ole life."

"Even without male companionship?"

She looked at me sharply, a darting, sly smile stretching her lips. "Ditching that baggage a couple years ago turned out to be part of the fun."

I stuck my toe in deeper. "And, with no replacement . . ."

She tossed her head back and laughed. "I replaced it. Did I say *it*?" She laughed harder. "I replaced *him* with happiness. Not a bad deal."

She leaned forward once again, folding her arms in her lap. She sat still for a moment, looking ahead, then unexpectedly began to cry.

I stood, went to her on the sofa and sat next to her. I placed my arms around her and held her tight. She sat stiffly.

"It's the damn wine," she said between sobs. "Every time I drink it without food I make a fool of myself." She stopped talking and sobbed some more. "I always think 'this time will be different,' but it never is. And I drink it anyway."

She looked at me, her face a cascade of tears.

"Is that crazy, or what?" she said. She brought her hands to her face and fought back her sobs.

"Some of the best times I've ever had were drinking wine and making a fool of myself."

She laughed through her waning tears and sat back. "Oh, that's a good joke. I needed a good joke. Thank you."

"That was a wisecrack, which wasn't all that funny. A joke is an amusing story with a punch line, or a humorous situation."

She laughed more. "Thank you, anyway." Tear tracks streaked her face, but she'd stopped sobbing. "You made me laugh, and I feel better."

"Crying and joking are good for the soul."

She swatted at me. "But you weren't joking, you were wisecracking." Her smile broadened.

She leaned over and softly kissed my cheek, her hair brushing my face, her body pressing against mine. The wine began reacting in me – quite differently than it appeared to in Juanita. I was glad for the moment that I didn't have to stand. Juanita lingered with her kiss and I placed my hand on her shoulder.

"I'm still not used to Marilyn's death," she said, keeping her lips close to my face, thrilling me with her warm breaths. "I try to keep it inside, but . . ."

"You don't have to explain. You've got to let it go, and that happens gradually. The wine just coaxed some out tonight, and that's okay."

She pulled back and looked at me. "I'd have said the same thing to someone else." She leaned against me once again.

As though a signal had been given, we both tilted away. We sat sideways on the sofa, facing each other. I glanced sidelong at our wine glasses on the table, both empty. They needed to stay that way.

"We didn't solve much tonight, did we?" Juanita said.

"No. But we learned some things, and that's always good."

"What did we learn?"

I didn't tell her that I'd learned she prudently applied her high-spirit and courage, a quality I found irresistibly attractive. Intoxicating. I'd also learned more how innocent and unpretentious she was, childlike in the most endearing way, and simply wonderful to be around. And, of course, I learned even more that she was undeniably – well, undeniably sexy. Hot.

"Aren't you going to tell me what we learned?" she asked. "Your mind seems to be elsewhere, at times."

"Sorry. I'm just thinking everything over," I quickly said, which wasn't altogether untrue. I just wasn't thinking what she thought I was thinking.

"Maybe we should stop talking about Marilyn and Roniece, and everything."

I couldn't have said it any better. "You're right. We'll sleep on it, let our respective subconscious' go to work and give us all the answers tomorrow morning."

"Sometimes you're happy to avoid things, aren't you?"

Whoa. A direct hit – right on the nose. "That comes from my stoic, northern European background." I'd had no clue where that remark came from.

Ah. Of course. The wine.

"I've always worn my heart on my sleeve," she said. "And my sense of humor, and my temper . . ."

"Temper? You?"

She grinned, her cheeks growing ever more rosy. "I'm Latina. Puerto Rican, to be exact. Everyone knows we're hot blooded, temperamental." Her eyes twinkled. "Passionate."

Give me the passion.

Damn, the wine again.

"I don't indulge stereotypical labeling," I said, smirking.

"You just labeled yourself. 'Northern European.' Stoic, and all that. But, the Irish are northern European, and I've heard that they're extroverted. Drunks, in fact."

"Point taken. I avoid some things because it's just me."

She grinned more broadly than ever, giggled, and reached for my hand. Her skin was warm. My racing, raging wine jag gathered speed, again piquing my carnal instincts, re-swelling my groin.

I leaned over her and picked up the wine bottle from the floor. "Here's your problem." I turned the bottle in my hands. "This is German wine. Why's a red-blooded Latina like you fooling around with a German?"

"They taste good. Sweet. And they're exciting."

"I wish I were German." I froze, staring at the bottle. Now, who's the wined-up fool?

"I'd always thought you were," she said, without missing a beat.

I stole a glance at her. She was still smiling, her eyes shining bright as stars.

Looking away, I said, "As a matter of fact, I am Irish. 'Blanchard' is an English name, but some of my ancestors had been conscripted into the English army and helped occupy Ireland and, so the story goes, defected and remained there. I guess they stayed for the booze."

"But, you're a stoic."

"A throw back to my Teutonic origins."

"Teutons are German, and you said you're not German."

"They're all out of same cage, really. Germans, English, Irish, Nordic. All had descended from the ancient Teutons, many tribes of which had interbred with invading Barbarians. Or been enslaved and ethnically cleansed. You know the Barbarians. Plunderers. Mass murderers."

I had no idea what I was talking about, but then I was a drunk, not an anthropologist.

"So, now you're a mass murderer?" she said, bending forward, intensifying what had become an almost constant giggle.

I laughed. "I did get far a field, didn't I?"

Far a field was where I wished to be, in a lush, lazy setting with Juanita. For the moment, the sofa had to do.

"You know," I said, "after drinking all this wine, I have to use the ah, the ah . . ."

"The can. The powder room is right over there." She pointed at a room in the hall next to the living room.

When I returned to the living room I noticed that Juanita had removed her shoes and curled her legs up under her. The lights were lowered. She turned her head to look at me, winked, and held out her hand. I took it and carefully stepped past her, to return to my place on the sofa. Before I could sit she tugged my hand, causing me to nearly sit on her. Her knee gently pressed against my thigh. She looked at me glassy-eyed. It wasn't from the wine and it wasn't from embarrassment at "making a fool" of herself.

My throat went dry. Blood pounded in my temples. I felt like a high school kid during his first encounter with the girl of his dreams. She held my gaze and parted her lips. A geyser of sexual desire erupted within me, much stronger than before.

Still holding my hand, Juanita arched her brow with a mock, puzzled expression. For a brief moment I tried remaining nonchalant, business-like.

"Well," I said nervously, "I guess I should be going."

She tugged my hand, pulling me closer.

I could overlook her encouragement no longer and, feeling like an amateur for hesitating, I leaned over and kissed her on the mouth. She'd lifted her head while I approached and kissed me back, passionately. Her lips were moist, her lipstick fresh and delicious. She parted her lips even more, the heat and moisture from her mouth radiated into mine. I withheld my tongue, still acting the amateur. Her warm, fluid tongue probed into my mouth and met mine. We melted into each other, remaining locked in a tight embrace.

We held our kiss, caressing each other. Parting briefly, I saw the look of rapture on her face, and knew I looked the same. We stayed on the couch for a long time, necking like teenagers. I hadn't felt the ecstasy of such intimacy with a woman for a long time. Too long. We parted again, showering each other's face and neck with kisses. Juanita held her arms around my neck, clearly not wanting to let go. I didn't want her to. I intertwined my fingers with thick clumps of her hair.

A decision had to be made.

As though she'd been reading my mind, she whispered, "What do we do now?"

The correct answer was easy. Saying it was difficult. "I think I should go home, for now," I said. "I want to do things right."

Still holding me around my neck, she smiled, and then dropped her head to my chest. "So do I."

After a few moments, we stood. She moved to me for a full-bodied embrace, pressing herself hard against me. I briefly considered asking if I could change my mind about leaving, but didn't. I brought my arm up behind her to look at my wristwatch – 11:45.

"I really should go," I said softly. "I can sleep a little later than you tomorrow morning."

"I'm all right. I'll make it to work."

"I want you to feel good tomorrow."

She looked up at me again, grinning. "I'll feel wonderful tomorrow."

"Me, too."

After dragging myself away from her lips, her embrace, her passion, I drove home, feeling powered by gossamer wings. We hadn't discussed anything about ourselves beyond that night, but we hadn't needed to. Something unstoppable had been put in motion. We'd figure out the details later. Before I knew it I was at home in bed, unable at first to sleep, from desire surging through my body and visions of Juanita surging through my head.

CHAPTER SIXTEEN

The flames of passion roaring through me finally died down, and I drifted off to sleep. The morning light was brighter than it usually was when I first awoke, yet I rolled over and went back to sleep. After waking with a start a short while later, I checked my radio clock – 8:05. My first thought was of Juanita. A thrill of ecstasy dashed through me when I recalled the previous night with her, and fantasies of future encounters flashed in my mind.

Within a few minutes, my phone rang. A strange urgency seemed attached to the ring. The feeling I had when I went to the kitchen to answer the phone will forever be with me. "Hello? Jack?" It was Juanita, speaking somewhat loud and shrill, her voice quivering.

"Good morning," I said cheerily, but anxiety rose in me. Something felt terribly wrong.

"I don't know how to tell you this," she said, and paused for a long moment.

I drew a deep breath. "Take your time. I'm shockproof." For a moment, I drained of all sensation, an ability I'd developed when I was a cop. "I've heard bad news before."

"L.C. Veasley was found dead in an alley early this morning. He'd been shot."

My resolve shattered. I pulled a chair out from the table and collapsed onto it. Nothing could have been more unexpected. Nothing could have thrown me deeper into shock. A cold, clammy sweat broke on my skin. I began shivering convulsively. My mind blanked at the same rate my stomach turned.

"Jack?" Juanita said. "Jack, are you there?"

"I'm here," I managed to whisper. My voice sounded distant, as though it weren't mine. My mind remained blank, my throat seized up.

"Are you okay, Jack?"

"I'm . . ." I swallowed. "I'm here. I mean I'm all right." For a brief time everything went numb again. I had no sense of time or where I was, or being on the phone with Juanita. I could feel the reality of L.C.'s murder closing in, a dark, swirling cloud filling the room all around me. I sat in the eye of a storm for a short while before being engulfed.

"What do you think this means for Roniece?" Juanita's question jolted me back to my senses.

"Christ, she's gotta be in trouble herself." For the moment I couldn't think of her further.

The looming, incapacitating haze of grief began swarming me. All at once I felt everything – the cold, the tears streaming down my face, the uncontrollable shaking. L.C. was dead. Unbelievable. He was too close to me, like my own blood, my own soul. I couldn't imagine him dead. The stone I felt growing in my chest would weigh on me forever.

I managed to speak. "The police should know about Roniece – I should call . . ." I lowered my head, brought my hand to my eyes.

"Wha' . . . ?"

I could no longer focus on Juanita's voice. "I need – I need some time. . . ."

Dropping the phone to the table, I leaned over with my head on my arm and fought back tears. My chest and stomach heaved. I began to retch, but with an empty stomach, there was nothing to puke.

"Jack?" I heard Juanita's voice from the telephone earpiece.

I took a moment to compose myself and brought the phone back to my ear. "I'm all right. It's taking me a moment to get a grip."

"I understand. You're in shock." After a pause, she asked, "Do you think L.C.'s murder somehow involves Roniece? Do you think she's in trouble? Or worse?"

"I have a bad feeling. L.C. doesn't always tell me everything he's up to. He's always had a tendency to do that. He may have gotten too close to the truth about her. Have you heard any more about his shooting?"

"He was found six blocks from City Hall, in an alley between Currie and Founder Streets."

"That's the worst neighborhood in the world. Nothing but drug houses and vacant lots. What the hell was he doing there by himself?"

"It's going around City Hall that the police believe they know how it happened, but of course, they aren't saying anything."

"They won't before they're ready."

"Do you think it might tie to Marilyn's murder? And any of this stuff with Roniece?"

"I don't see how it can't."

"Isn't there anything you can do to find out more? No one you can talk to at the police department?"

"I'm afraid not."

An excited woman's voice sounded in the background on the phone. I couldn't hear what she said. "I have to go, Jack. There are detectives here in City Hall, interviewing everyone. People are terribly upset." The woman in the background continued talking loudly. Juanita hung up before she could explain why the police were there.

What the hell was going on with the mass police interviews at City Hall? Certainly, they were related to L.C.'s shooting, but how? Curiosity chiseled through my grief. My thinking cap would shield me from deep pain for at least a while, and I yanked it on tightly. L.C. was found shot in an alley early this morning. He must have found something out about Roniece's situation – maybe she'd finally opened up to him. Then he made a boneheaded move – damn him – and confronted a killer. My fear was that Roniece would also be found dead somewhere.

But there was always the chance that he would've called me.

Dammit! My cell phone.

I'd turned the son of a bitch off the day before and never turned it back on. The red light had been steady on my home answering machine when I woke up. I quickly went to my bedroom and got the cell phone from my dresser, turned it on, and checked my voice mail. One message, at 5:23 p.m., the day before. Holding my breath,

I entered my voice mail and listened. . . .

Street noise, cars going past. L.C. saying, "Jack? Are you there? Pick up. Jack? Goddammit." He'd hung up. Why hadn't he tried calling back? He wasn't found dead until almost 12 hours later. He'd obviously wanted me in on whatever he was up to, and would have kept trying. At least, I'd thought so. But he could be unpredictable, hot headed, and impatient. He *would* have moved on his own if he were pissed off enough. I'd have to call the police right away. His message may have been the last known contact he'd had with anyone before his murder.

I called the police and asked for Will Tandy of the Homicide Squad. The same female officer as before answered the main phone line. Good luck prevailed. Tandy was working and in the office. Within moments he was on the phone.

"What's up, Jack?" he asked.

"I might know something about the murder in the alley between Currie and Founder." After explaining the basics about my relationship with L.C. – as well as how close we'd been personally – and Roniece Veasley, Tandy assured me they'd start looking for Roniece immediately.

"I brought her photo and record up on my computer while we've been talking," he said. "Petty thief, petty drug offenses. She's on probation."

"I assume you've already searched L.C.'s house?"

"Yeah. No one was there."

"Then I'd go to 2026 North 14th Street. A hooker named Colette lives there – calls herself 'Mina,' in case you want to check her out with the Vice Squad. Roniece has stayed there from time to time."

"We'll start there and knock down every door in the whole damn city, if we have to. This is a bigger deal than anyone can imagine. You'll hear the details soon enough."

I wasn't surprised. The potential for an ever-expanding scandal and violence had obviously existed since the beginning – the way Marilyn Chase had predicted.

"I'll be at my cell number if you think I can help any more," I said, and we hung up.

Within seconds I realized I was once again on my own – no

further need for my thinking cap, nothing to do, nowhere to hide. Tears welled in my eyes.

I wiped my eyes with my arm. I stayed dry for a brief time, and then the flooding started all over. It was strange, I wasn't even thinking about L.C. I couldn't afford to.

Getting showered and dressed helped occupy my mind, but the stone I'd felt in my chest continued to grow. I needed to keep busy, and avoid news reports on radio or TV. The morning newspaper had been printed before the story of L.C.'s murder had been reported, but I didn't read it anyway.

There was only one story.

I decided to try walking to clear my head. It didn't feel like a good idea, but I pushed myself to go. I hooked my cell phone to my belt, but before I got to my rear door the phone rang. I expected it to be Juanita.

"Jack?" I recognized Detective Tandy's voice when I answered.

"Would you be able to come to my office?" he said. "There's some things I'd like to go over with you."

He had a strange tone in his voice.

"Sure," I said. "When do you want me there?"

"Now would be convenient."

I agreed, and headed toward the garage and my car. I couldn't imagine why Tandy wanted to see me so quickly, but I was too dazed to think about it. But it did occur to me that Tandy had been making more than a request when he said he wanted me to come "now."

In a short while I found myself in the Detective Bureau waiting room at police headquarters. The room had been remodeled since I'd worked there, including the addition of comfortable sofas and chairs, a large screen TV, two fancy floor lamps, and cushy carpeting. A large end table before me held a stack of magazines, which I leisurely picked through. Newsweek, Time, Ladies' Home Journal, Sports Illustrated. The usual. And the not-so-usual, Tactical Weaponry, a slick, "self-defense" publication. It hadn't been addressed to the police department, which wasn't surprising – it wouldn't have been allowed. Must have been added to the stack by someone interested in educating the public on his or her style of self-defense.

I chose that one to look at. I was familiar with the subject, which was technical but not challenging. First, there were guns. Lots and lots of guns. Full-page photographs also showed military types posing with all manner of weaponry, gear, and clothing. Winter outfits. Underwater outfits. You-name-it outfits, including those used for "special operations." Wet work, the British had named it. Dark jumpsuits, light jumpsuits, jungle and desert camouflaged jumpsuits.

And more guns.

Of course, the obligatory ninja suit was prominently featured. A black, loose fitting garment, it sported bulging pockets on the pants, chest and sleeves. The model in the photo also wore a ninja mask. The suit, along with everything else, was really neat stuff. But average people don't need the type of weaponry and the clothing displayed. This magazine was clearly geared to Montana militia types.

A medium to large caliber handgun will do for self-defense.

I studied the ninja suit photo and read the sales pitch. My brain began to unlock, and for the first time, I had that special feeling I get when I have a good hunch. It was just a spark, it needed fleshing out, but it seemed right.

A female clerk opened the door to Detective Bureau and stepped into the waiting room. "Detective Tandy will see you now."

I dropped the magazine to the table and stood, put my hunch to the back of mind, and walked to the door. The clerk guided me through a narrow hallway to a small cubicle, and I sat in an arm-less, straight-backed wooden chair. The room, assembled with beige metal, portable walls, had no windows and barely enough space for the chair I sat on, a desk, and a file cabinet. A moment later I heard Detective Tandy's booming voice in the hallway, approaching the room.

He entered, offered me his hand and said, "Hi, Jack," as though he'd known me forever, then sat on an old, creaky wooden swivel chair behind the desk. A tall, rawboned man, he was trim and tough looking. He wore a long-sleeved white shirt with the cuffs rolled up his forearms, a black tie loosened at the collar, and dark slacks.

"I bet you'd like to know why I asked you to come in right away," he said. His loud, full voice seemed to vibrate the room. His large head with dark, wavy hair combed back, bore a face that had seen serious acne wars, with craters and bumps everywhere. The skin disorder badly marred an otherwise handsome face.

"Your eyes are red and puffy," he said. "Allergies?"

"Yeah, allergies."

He knew damn well that I felt extremely bad about L.C.'s death. He was being tactful, allowing a man to save face. That's how it is in the macho world of the streets – men who cry are sissies, and cops have to know how to play a guy.

"You explained how close you and L.C. were, and this has been rough on you," he said, in a sincere tone. "But there's stuff we need to cover."

"I'll tell you everything I know," I said. "I just hope you find Roniece – that she's still healthy."

He withdrew a yellow legal pad from the desk drawer and placed it on the desktop. "Me, too."

He prepared to take notes, and I gave him the same thumbnail sketch of Roniece's activities as I'd known them from the day she first took off, as well as L.C.'s strange phone message on my cell phone the evening before. I also disclosed details of the information I'd gotten about the Earl Jones alley murder, as well as Four Dead's shooting case two years ago. I didn't mention going to Marilyn's house – with the police having investigated the burglary and seeing me there, he'd have already known that.

A knowing look grew on his face. "I know you've also been sniffing around City Hall." He made a sly smile.

"Strictly business."

He raised his hand. "Oh, I know." He looked down at his notes. "Just like checking out Marilyn Chase's house with, ah, with your 'partner.' We'll have to see how L.C.'s phone message figures."

"What about Roniece?"

"We're beating the bushes for her now."

I frowned. He was too casual. It seemed as though he already knew everything I told him. The swivel chair squeaked when he sat back, crossing one leg over the other, and staring at me with eyes that belonged on a pit bull. He wasn't dismissing me, but he wasn't pressing the interview.

After an awkward pause, I said, "So, do you know who killed L.C.?" If he could keep me on ice, he could be asked questions he didn't want to answer.

He remained relaxed. "Actually, we've got things to work with."

"Like what?"

He sat forward and looked down. He sighed. He tapped his fingers on the desktop. Looking up at me with softer eyes, he said, "A witness saw L.C. going into City Hall early last evening, just before six o'clock."

Whoever L.C. went to see at City Hall was at least somehow linked to his killing, sure as shit. Anyone would at least guess that. Given Tandy's comment about my activities at City Hall, it was strange he didn't ask me more about my association with people there. He'd get to it soon enough.

I forced a smile and asked, "Do you have any suspects, or are you still working on it?"

His eyes narrowed. For a moment he looked disgusted, but quickly blanked his expression. "Yeah. We're looking hard at somebody." He stood. "Can you wait here a minute? I've got to make a call."

Bullshit, he had to make a call. I looked at my watch. If he didn't return within ten minutes, and I was being generous, I'd walk out. People walked past in the hallway outside the room. I fidgeted in my chair. The drama that I knew was building around me couldn't sink in. My feelings were growing duller than a lecture on economics. My eyes burned. I palmed surging moisture from them.

Five minutes after he'd left, Detective Tandy returned to the room and sat back down behind the desk. "Where were we?" he asked casually.

The scene seemed scripted, with only Tandy knowing the lines. "I asked if you had any suspects."

"Oh, yeah." He sat back again, his chair growing more annoying with every creak. "We're thinking in a certain direction."

"Really?" I was surprised he shared that with me.

"Yeah. It's going to be a big surprise."

The inkling I'd had while looking at the photo in the magazine in the waiting room returned. I dared not think the name that first popped into my mind – that would be my own surprise. Besides, I didn't want to jinx anything.

Tandy had remained quiet.

"But you're not going to tell me who it is," I said.

He didn't answer. His brow lines bunched together in a well-worn pattern, a roadmap of his mind when in deep thought. He lifted his head and stared off. His expression soured, as though listening to the sound of finger nails scraping a chalkboard.

Without looking at me, he asked, "You still have good rapport with that dude in prison, Four Dead?"

"What?"

"Crazy boy, counting pock marks on his cell bricks."

I felt defensive. Tandy hadn't earned the right to talk that way about Four Dead. But then, cops have been exposed to too much, and generalizing doesn't only come easy, it is very often necessary.

"Yeah. I think so." I felt my face flush. He was playing me, and I didn't like it.

Tandy's face went blank once again and he looked me directly in the eye. "We know there was a third guy against Four Dead in his shootout. The guy ran off and we never found him. We never identified him."

I was stunned. My vision of "rapport" with Four Dead clouded over. I realized that Tandy's wrenching switch to Four Dead had exposed a link from the City Hall mess all the way back to the Earl Jones murder. Maybe the connection was only Tandy's theory, maybe it was more. I knew one thing – he'd never tell me.

I played him right back. "The third guy wasn't mentioned in the police report. So, the reason you're telling me this is . . . ?"

He sniffed, he sighed, he squirmed in his chair, a clumsily done act, and said, "You know why, and I expect that you'll look into it." After a moment, he said, "And you're gonna find out who we suspect in L.C.'s shooting soon, anyway. It's a city councilman. Hayward Artic."

My eyes bugged. My jaw dropped. Yet another stunning surprise, quite different from my own suspicion.

"How'd you come up with that? You got a witness, or . . ."

Tandy smiled slightly. "That's a long story," he said with a tease in his voice.

Something must have come up between my first conversation

with him and then. Why he'd called me in – and why he'd given me any information at all about L.C.'s murder – puzzled me. Another possibility besides Artic entered my mind – perhaps it was whomever the hell Roniece had seen at the Summerfest grounds.

Artic and drugs and his daughter and Earl Jones. And Roniece and Four Dead, all somehow linking to the Mayor McCord and Marilyn Chase, and now, L.C. Veasley. The players couldn't have been more diverse.

The phone rang. "Detective Tandy," Tandy said after picking the receiver on the first ring. "He is? Good. We're ready."

He hung up. The pit bull glare returned to his eyes and he said, "Someone else wants to see you. Come with me."

We both stood and I followed him to the elevators in the hallway outside the Detective Bureau.

CHAPTER SEVENTEEN

We entered an empty elevator, the first car to arrive at our floor. I didn't care where we were going, or who I was to see. It felt good to drift numbly and I savored it, knowing it wouldn't last. The elevator stopped on the sixth floor, one from the top. The doors slid open and we entered the hallway. Unauthorized personnel had no access to this level, unless accompanied by a police officer. There were only administrative offices here, as well as on the seventh floor above.

I followed Detective Tandy into a room with a steel door at the far end of the hallway. Despite my number of years on the force and working in this building, I'd never been in that room. After entering I stood in a narrow, semi-dark hall, with Tandy beside me.

"Go in there," he said, pointing toward a door several steps from where we were.

I went forward. Tandy did not accompany me. I pushed the door open and entered a large, wood-paneled room. A highly polished circular wood table sat in the center, surrounded by a dozen overstuffed swivel chairs. The lights were off and the sun dimly shone through a bank of tinted windows on one side of the room.

On the far side of the table sat Chief Jerome Rhodes, wearing his white police shirt. His navy blue blazer was slung over a chair next to him, his hat placed on top. Gold military-style trappings decorated his shirt. My eyes were drawn to his gold chief's badge, pinned above the left shirt pocket. Even in this subdued setting, his accessories were impressive.

He smiled. "Hi, Jack. Glad you could come so soon."

I felt uneasy again. I didn't answer. What could he possibly want with me? I'd certainly been displaying a bewildered look. He smiled more broadly.

He stood, grabbed his coat and hat, and slung them over his arm. "Come on, let's go up to my office."

He turned and stepped toward the wall behind him and pushed on a panel, which swung open like a door. He went through the opening and I walked around the table to follow him into an ill-lighted stairwell, with a staircase that led upward to a door at the upper landing.

"Never knew about this, did you?" he said casually, without looking back. "Leads to my office."

I still hadn't spoken. He didn't seem to care. He appeared to be enjoying the game he was playing, and his little mystery tour. It was off-putting – he'd never acted that way toward me from the day I'd met him. He began walking up the stairs, with less spring in his step than he normally had. His head was down. His shoulders sagged. Apparently, he wasn't enjoying himself so much, after all.

Our out-of-rhythm footsteps scraped the steps while we walked up. The walls were cement block painted gray, making the stairwell look like a prison cell. At last we entered his office through what I'd always thought was a closet door on the wall on opposite side of the room from his desk. I'd been in the Police Chief's office a number of times when I was a cop, once with then-Detective Jerry Rhodes when the chief at that time presented us with a meritorious citation for a homicide we'd solved. But I'd always come in through the front door.

We stepped into an area of the room with a long sofa and some cushioned chairs. The chief's desk lay beyond. Criminal law and other reference books filled mahogany wood shelving behind his desk, which reached from a built in credenza to the ceiling. The room looked the same as it did the last time I saw it.

After walking half way to his desk he turned and shook my hand. "Good to see you, again, Jack." His face was drawn, with worry lines appearing almost as fractures, as though all the stress of the world had landed there.

"Good to see you too, Jerry." I called him by his first name without thinking. "I mean, Chief." He turned and continued walking toward his desk without reacting.

"Sit down," he said, pointing at one of two cushy maroon leather chairs positioned in front of his desk. He walked behind his desk and draped his coat over the back of a plush, high-backed, maroon leather swivel chair. He sat in the chair, placed his hat on the side of the desktop, drew in a deep breath, held it, and let it out with a long whoosh.

"I'd ask how you're doing," I said after sitting, "but to be honest, chief, you look a little, a little tired."

"It's Jerry, Jack. Or even Dusty, for chrissakes. I'm tired of hearing 'Chief, Chief, Chief,' all fucking day."

"You haven't changed. That's good."

He sat forward, leaned his elbows on his desk, and said, "I've got a problem. Some people want you to have a problem, too." He looked at me, his laser eyes searing holes through me, the way they did everyone.

"Must be a helluva weird problem if you're calling *me* in for a private talk."

He continued, as though he hadn't heard me. "Two murders connected to City Hall, and the police haven't officially solved them yet. If that doesn't change – and change *now* – the next sound you'll hear will be great wailing and gnashing of teeth. And the word has spread through some channels that a PI is sticking his nose in – trying to screw things up. How's that for a helluva problem?"

I affected a surprised expression. "You don't mean me, do you?"

He held my gaze for a long, awkward moment. I could almost hear him thinking. . . . "Who the fuck else would I mean, wise ass?"

"What about the mayor?" I asked, after it became clear he wouldn't answer my first question. "You're trying to finger him for killing Marilyn Chase. And a little bird told me you're looking at Hayward Artic for L.C. Veasley's killing last night."

He waved his hand. "Capers in progress aren't capers solved, you know. Charges issued by the D.A. are what count."

My suspicions had been correct – the mayor hadn't been slam-dunked yet, and they still had their work cut out for them with Artic.

I decided to make no comment.

"You think I'm trying to mess up your murder investigations," I said, my sarcasm showing a wee bit. "And you know I'm the PI they're talking about, even though you haven't said it."

"No, I don't think you're trying to mess up my murder investigations. But people are panicky, looking for scapegoats. Looking to get someone. A head on a platter draws attention, gives the rats time to scurry for cover."

"Scurry from what, if they've nothing to hide?"

He smirked and tilted his head, looking as though I should know exactly what he meant. "Exposure. Politicians – and anyone in a high profile position of power – all have things to hide, and they know they could have their stomach contents examined, from the bottom up. That's uncomfortable. They could be found out if they're dirty in any way, and there could be accompanying, unintended consequences. You know? There's other examples I could use, but you get my drift."

"Of course. All of that goes without saying."

He snorted softly and shook his head. "Of course. Anyway, you're not in that tangled web, are you?"

I felt more at ease. He wasn't one of those out to get me, or it would already have been a *fait accompli.* "No, I'm not. So, who's been dropping my name?"

He raised his hand toward me. "Who do you think?"

Vincent Dragos, of course. He didn't like me. He'd run to the principal. "Some pissant detective who powders the mayor's ass." I shifted in my chair. "What do you want from me, aside from getting the hell out of Dodge."

"What makes you think I want something from you?"

I smiled. "Jerry. It's me, Jack. I'd already be gone if you wanted to dispense with me. And you wouldn't bring me up here just to chat."

He slapped both hands on the table, made a fake grimace, and sat back. "Okay. On the level. From the day you first met with Juanita Velez, you've been tracked. Your whole involvement has been noted. My guess is you're too close to the truth, at least about *something* bad, and someone's gettin' antsy. The whole ball of wax has been kicked up to my desk."

"You know everything?"

"I'm the chief. What do you think? And I know you well enough to know that if there's a chance of you unearthing the truth, or other 'unintended consequences,' it'll happen. That's all I really need to know about your involvement."

"What would be wrong with that?"

"There's more here than murder and investigating, and stuff. It's political. People have joined forces at City Hall, and have asked that you be invited off the premises. There are people who wonder what you and Ms. Velez were doing at Marilyn Chase's house last night."

I shifted in my seat. "I – Ms. Velez and I – explained ourselves to the officers at the scene."

"Cagey doesn't fly with me," he said impatiently, "just like it wouldn't fly with you. But I'm not gonna come right out and ask what you were doing there. Just like I'm not gonna ask why you're following up on two separate drug related murders from two years ago, and chasing Roniece Veasley around, who keeps trying to make herself disappear, and what *her* involvement might be.

"And I'm not gonna ask why you think there could be a link between those drug murders and Marilyn Chase's murder. Or why you probably think there's a link between all of this and L.C. Veasley's murder last night. And there's more I'm not gonna go into."

I was stunned. Besides knowing everything I was up to, he'd taken the time to precisely string together both my ideas and probable conclusions. If anyone but Jerry Rhodes had put it to me that way, I'd have told him or her they had it wrong. I couldn't do that with him. But I didn't take his bait.

"Doesn't matter what I think," I said. "The mayor killed Marilyn Chase, and Hayward Artic killed L.C. Cases closed."

He leaned back, looking slightly surprised. But he didn't take my bait, either. "As I've indicated, those matters are under consideration." He let out a deep sigh and stared off, his eyes narrowing, the corners of his mouth turning downward.

He was really feeling pressure. If the police couldn't pin the mayor for Marilyn Chase and couldn't solve L.C.'s murder, or at least get City Hall off the hook, certain people would bring a wooden cross, sized for Jerry Rhodes, along with rusty spikes and a sledgehammer, to the Police Administration Building.

I stared at him intently while letting everything soak in.

"What?" he asked.

"Oh, nothing. I'm glad you're not asking my take on any of this, Jerry, because I couldn't give you a good answer. I've only got hunches. Of course, everybody's got hunches, even people who don't know diddly."

He flattened his lips, raised his eyebrows, and breathed out heavily through his nose. He was disappointed. He'd hoped I had something to tell him.

I wanted to draw him farther out. "So, anyway, I guess I'll leave it all alone. I mean, that's what you and everyone else wants."

"I'm in a position," he said weakly.

Here it comes. "What does that mean?"

"You're supposed to be a bug splat on my windshield when you leave this room. And officially, you will be."

I hesitated. "And unofficially?"

His grave look faded, and he smiled wanly. "You know, there's a whole heap of rules. Everywhere you go – rules, rules, rules."

He opened a desk drawer and brought out an engraved wooden humidor, opened it and took out one obviously expensive cigar.

"I know you don't smoke," he said while clipping the cigar's tip.

He put the box away, brought the cigar to his nose, and sniffed deeply. He spoke and moved slowly, making the kind of grand production only he could make.

"You know, there's a city ordinance against smoking in this building," he said. "I've endorsed it, and I've enforced it. People have gotten tickets for violating that law." He looked at me expectantly while putting the cigar in his mouth.

He'd always been a dramatic son of a bitch.

Majestically, he picked up an ornamental cigarette lighter from his desktop, sparked a flame, and brought it to the tip of the cigar. After drawing in the flame, blue smoke puffed from the corners of his mouth. The expensive cigar's expensive aroma drifted to me. He continued puffing heartily, put the lighter back on the desk, and looked at me.

I said, "Rules were made to be broken, I guess."

Eyeing me steely, he rotated the cigar with his fingers and thumb between his lips, withdrew it, and said, "Remember how police officers are allowed to violate certain laws in order to do their job? You know, drive a squad car through a red light while responding to an emergency?"

I understood perfectly. "I believe that's one of the things I recall about police work, yes."

"You've always been a sarcastic son of a bitch, haven't you?"

I smiled. "We were the perfect team. I was Mr. Inside, with my smart mouth, and you were Mr. Outside, with your smoothness and your metaphors. How's your cigar?"

"Better with every puff."

He could see that he had me, and knew that not only would I end-run the jackals for him, I'd work even harder. But it was time for me to change the subject.

"Is your office bugged?" I asked.

He coughed out a blue cloud of smoke and sat up as though yanked forward by an unseen string. He snorted a laugh of sorts. His face turned red. He sat back and stared at me, his eyes twinkling.

I sat still, keeping a straight face. "I'm gonna guess that means no. Good. I don't want you to get into trouble for smoking in the building."

Still smiling, he again sat forward. He continued taking steady, deep puffs on the cigar.

"Why don't you come back to the force?" he asked. "We can be partners again."

It was my turn to laugh. "By what magic could you make that happen?"

"I'd pull strings to get you rehired as a detective, and demote myself *back* to detective. We'd ride into the sunset together."

"In case you haven't noticed, I'm already beyond the sunset. And the way things are going, *you* should join *me*."

The twinkle left his eyes. I felt bad. I should have let him stay in his little reverie.

"At least you got to laugh a little," I said. "Your mood brightened."

He waved his hand. "It wasn't meant to last."

Since he was going to use me, I had use for him, also. "It'd sure be convenient to know what was found missing from Marilyn's house during the burglary."

"You know what was taken."

"No, I don't. How the hell would I?"

I truly didn't know, although I had a suspicion.

He swiveled back and forth in his chair, put his cigar in an ashtray, slumped and folded his hands over his lap. "Same thing that was stolen from her office."

What the hell was stolen from her office? I held my breath while collecting myself. "Oh," I said, as casually as I could. "That's interesting."

The chief had overestimated my inside information. Or, maybe he hadn't. He could be Machiavellian, not beyond twisting scenarios and passing cryptic clues until his message was understood.

"Juanita Velez had been assigned by City Hall officials to check Marilyn's office after the police had searched it," I said, trying to see in which direction he'd take me. "She said a computer monitor was missing from her office."

He'd slouched deeper in his chair, in which he continued twisting back and forth. He slid his gaze to me. He arched his brow, widened his eyes, and nodded his head ever so slightly.

"Yes," I said. "That's very interesting."

"Yes, it is." He stood quickly and stuck his hand out.

I stood also and reached out to shake his hand. "It was good to talk, Jerry. Maybe we'll speak again."

"Don't stay a stranger," he said, while reaching toward me and clasping my hand in a firm shake. "I mean I really hope to hear from you someday. Someday soon."

He came around the table and while we embraced, he discretely placed a business card in my shirt pocket. I left his office, this time through the front door.

CHAPTER EIGHTEEN

I'd been lost in time. My strange meeting with Chief Rhodes had drawn me away from my pain. The moment I stepped from his office, reality worked me over once again. A vision of L.C.'s corpse opened wide on an autopsy table came and went through my mind. The ache of grief and depression quickly followed, tightening around me like a python's coils. I'd hoped relief awaited me while I stepped into the brightly lighted main hallway, but nothing had changed. I walked toward the elevators, intending to return to the Detective Bureau waiting room.

The chief's expression of no confidence in solving either the Marilyn Chase or the L.C. Veasley homicides had been more disturbing than surprising. Clumsily committed, high profile crimes such as these usually have loose ends pointing, however shakily, toward the perpetrators. I couldn't be exactly sure what he had in these two cases, but it was obvious the connections weren't heading toward each other just yet.

Learning from Detective Tandy that there'd been a third participant in Four Dead's shooting who'd run away – albeit still unidentified and unlocated – would normally have been number one on my list of Important Discoveries for the Day. Chief Rhodes had to have been in on having Tandy slip that information to me, but how could finding that person assist me in working on the City Hall crimes? For the moment, it didn't matter.

The elevator arrived and I stepped on to go down.

The police and D.A.'s office were buying time with their impending charges against the mayor. And while there may have been arrows pointing at Hayward Artic, there was no indication that anyone was ready to loose the bowstring. I decided that the lack of information and instructions was my cue to work things my own way, especially after the chief and his illegal cigar smoke had given me the go-ahead to be involved at all.

Once off the elevator and back inside the Detective Bureau waiting room, I grabbed the Tactical Weaponry magazine from the table and walked out with it. No one else had been in the room, but that wouldn't have stopped me, anyway. I rolled up the magazine and carried it as though it were mine, and left the building.

My destination was set in my mind, and I nearly ran to my car in the parking lot across from the police building. The excitement I began to feel neutralized the shock and discouragement brought by L.C.'s murder. The bindings of depression had loosened their grip. The warrior's instincts I'd developed during my cop days resurfaced, the old automatic pilot took over.

So, Four Dead had forgotten to tell me about another man being involved with his shootout. That would make for an interesting conversation. If I learned a name – and if my latest hunch gleaned from the pages of a wacky militia magazine were correct – I might actually be on the way to solving an old murder. If I learned the truth about that, there was a chance I could wend my way forward and find some clues about who killed Marilyn Chase and L.C. Veasley.

Alas, truth and proof are not always synonymous in criminal matters, but I'd worry about that later.

It was early afternoon. I drove to the outskirts of town, which quickly lead to a familiar, serene stretch of country highway toward the state prison. I felt removed from time once again, my heartbeat jack hammering in my chest, my adrenals pumping fire through my veins. I glanced several times at the magazine lying on the passenger seat next to me, even patted it once or twice. At times I drove 20 miles an hour over the speed limit, unconcerned about getting a ticket.

At last I pulled into the prison parking lot. After calling the prison office, I verified that Four Dead was available for an interview.

In my excitement, I'd done things ass backward by going to the prison first, and I could have been denied permission. I wouldn't have cared. The drive had kicked out the jams.

Soon I found myself seated once again on a cold concrete stool in front of a bulletproof window in the prisoner interview area. I'd brought the militia magazine with me. While waiting for the guards to bring Four Dead, my confidence sagged. Even if he said everything I wanted to hear, how could I proceed to connect the dots? I had grave doubts that the police – or I – would ever have the physical evidence necessary to solve the Earl Jones, et al., murder. Never mind wending my way toward any other murder investigations.

Four Dead appeared before me, accompanied by a guard. He looked healthier than either of the last times I'd seen him.

"You look like hell," he said to me. "The grim reaper chasin' you?" He had a gleam in his eye and a smirk on his face. "You bein' too much a dick, pissin' people off?"

He almost seemed happy to see me. I forced a smile. "I'm always too much of a dick, Four Dead."

"They out to get you now, huh."

"They got me, Four Dead. Had me a long time ago."

He threw his head back and laughed. "Must be what you deserve."

My smile scuttled from my face. I breathed in and out heavily. "L.C.'s dead. He was shot in an alley in town last night."

Four Dead's expression soured, his brow knit into a web of confusion. He stared at me, past me, uncomprehending. "Who did it?" he asked. "L.C. chased too many dope dealers around lookin' for Roniece, didn't he?"

"I don't know who did it, although the police are supposed to have a lead. And I think L.C. only chased one dope dealer, but it was one dope dealer too many."

"Damn," Four Dead said, the color fading from his face. "What about Roniece." He crossed his arms in his lap and rocked forward and back.

"She came back home, but she's missing again, since before L.C. got shot, and the cops are beatin' every bush. Draggin' every swamp."

He continued rocking, a lost look in his eyes. "You think she dead?"

"I hope she's just hiding some more."

He stopped rocking and again looked at me. "Why you here? I don't know nothin' 'bout it."

"Easy, Four Dead. There's a couple things to discuss."

"Yeah, dick. They always one mo' thang they want to discuss." He spoke in a forced twang, edged with disgust.

I brought my thumb and forefinger to the bridge of my nose and looked down, then again palmed away excess moisture forming in my eyes. No way would I betray my broken heart.

"Goddamn," Four Dead said. "You and L.C. that close?"

Too late. "Yeah."

I gave him as hard a look as I could muster, and began by opening the magazine to the page and photograph I wanted him to see. I showed the photo to him. "What do you see?"

He leaned forward, studied the picture for a moment, and then forced a mirthless laugh. "You know what 'dat is," he said while alternately looking at the picture and me. He leaned back.

I'd shown him the photo of the man in the ninja suit. "How close is this picture to the man you saw the night Earl Jones and everybody were shot?" He hadn't actually admitted being there, but I knew this would draw him out.

He hesitated, making a production of the moment. Looking at me with half-hooded eyelids, he said, "It the same."

"Is it what you'd call a ninja suit?"

"It what the fuck *is* a ninja suit. What 'dat magazine?"

"A militia magazine. They sell the same kind of stuff to regular people that the military uses. Special shit, too, like ninja suits."

"Regular people buyin' ninja suits, and tanks an' poison gas, an' shit? Ain't that crazy?"

"Easy, Four Dead. Your gang would love to get their hands on this stuff. But it's expensive. You can make up your own version of some things in this magazine, especially clothing."

"Wasn't no made up version *dat* ninja dude had on. That fo' sure."

My heart raced. Surging adrenaline blotted out my gloominess.

"Can you still see the image of that night in your mind? Can you see all the details?"

"It a picture."

"Right. A portrait, in fact. Sometimes a film, or a video. Created by you."

He smiled and waved his hand. "They makin' me do my meds all the time, now. I still see it if I want, but I know what it is."

"Medication clears you all up, huh?"

He closed his eyes and shook his head. "It ain't like 'dat. I can't explain."

"But you can remember the things that played Punch and Judy in your head when you were off drugs. Right?"

"Punchin' *who*?"

"It's from the culture of a long time ago, in a country far, far away."

"Wha'?"

"Nothing. Could you see that image now, if you wanted to?"

He hesitated, looking at me strangely. "Uh-huh."

"And you're sure you see a real ninja suit, not somethin' made up. Right?"

"Uh-huh."

Obviously not evidence, but enough to inspire me to further my pursuit.

I closed the magazine and rolled it up. "There's another thing I need to discuss."

He sat still and silent, adopting the posture of a cowering animal.

"How come you never mentioned the third guy who attacked you during the shooting? It's not even in the police report, although they know about it."

He smiled and made a sly laugh. "Dude runs before it started. No reason to talk about it. 'Sides, he could say shit dat'd buried my ass forever."

That made sense. The third man could certainly have testified against him, and hurt him badly.

"Did the cops ask you about him?"

"Right after they arrested me, yeah. But I denied it."

"Okay, okay," I said. "But things have changed, and I ain't the cops. What's his name?"

He wouldn't answer.

"Come on, Four Dead. He couldn't hurt you any more. He doesn't have to know who told me."

"Street names is all I know. He work for Jones, and he know Roniece. Surprised me, him bein' wid' 'dem dudes I stanked."

"And his street name is?"

"Was Pimp Man, 'den. I hears it different now."

It had probably become different a dozen times since the shooting. Some of the gangstas change their street names more often that a hooker changes sex partners – especially if they have something like this dogging their past.

"Last I hear is Ray-Ray," Four Dead said. "He visit a brother up here. Came a couple weeks ago."

"Who'd he see? He had to have signed in."

Four Dead held his hands palms up, and shrugged. "Don't know. You'll have to dig on it."

"Fair enough. Who knows? I may find the answers, and it'll be you who clears up all this murder."

"Man, you crazy."

"I know. But that don't mean I won't figure things out, and that it ain't because of what you've kept in your head these past two years."

I stood to leave. He pushed a button next to him on the wall and I heard the rattling of keys and chains and a guard coming closer.

"You catch the bad guys, you think the D.A.'ll cut me some slack?"

I hadn't yet thought of that. "I'll be damn sure and mention it, Four Dead."

The guard came while he stood, and began leading him away.

After I turned away, he yelled – "Hey, don't forget to mention my real name to the D.A. – 'Reginald Thackery'."

I turned back and saw him standing next to the guard, smiling, and pointing both forefingers at me. Then he gave a double thumbs up, and the guard led him away

Seeing Four Dead doing well had lifted my spirits. I hoped he stayed on his meds.

Walking back outside into the bright sunlight brought the return of my dark mood. I tried blowing it off by thinking that Four Dead had said exactly what I'd hoped he would, that I had at least a chance of uncovering – of proving – the truth. It didn't work, at least not right away.

I forced myself to think of nothing else on the way back to town. Incredible – even the remote possibility of a locked up, schizo crackhead, ringing down the curtain not only on murder in the streets but also at City Hall. You never know. You just never know. Then again, what normal person would be likely to have firsthand knowledge of murder and such things? A Harvard College professor?

It was later than I'd thought – after 4:30. For the first time since receiving the horrible news about L.C. that morning, I thought of and kept my thoughts on Juanita. I grabbed the phone from the glove box and saw that there were no messages, which made me anxious. I'd thought she might have called. She'd probably been embroiled with the mess at City Hall.

I obeyed the speed limit on the way back to town. Depressing thoughts about L.C. began bleeding into my mind, intruding on my efforts to focus on solving murders, and day dreaming about Juanita. I turned on the radio news and heard a woman's voice battling static to tell me the latest stories. I was still too far from the city, and I decided let it go until I called Juanita.

Arriving home and entering my apartment brought more angst. Four calls had been forwarded to my answering machine, all from attorneys on old cases. I gave them a different phone number than anyone else – the last thing I needed was a whiny-assed call from a lawyer while I was doing something important.

The messages reminded me of what I'd really been all those years as a PI – an errand boy. I'd mostly covered bases with a thousand previous cleat marks, and allowed people to close their files for good. At least I'd made decent money.

At 6:00 my phone rang. "How are you?" Juanita said, almost breathlessly, when I answered. "I thought you might call me back today." She sounded apprehensive.

"I got busy. Busy with things you wouldn't believe. I'd like to see you."

"Why don't you come to my house?" Her whispery voice affected me like that of a Siren.

"Well, I should eat and clean up. . . ."

"Come now. I need your company." Her voice caught. She softly wept for a moment.

"I'll be there as soon as I can."

I cleaned up and grabbed a bite to eat anyway, then went to Juanita's house. She presented a comforting sight when she opened her door. Her mane of dark hair fell partly down her chest and shoulders, over the white cloth top she was wearing. When I stepped in she hugged me tightly around my neck, as though she needed saving from drowning. A pleasant floral scent infused her still damp, shampooed hair.

She quickly let go and led me by the hand to her living room. To me she looked spectacular in her white top that reached to an inch above the waistband of her blue jean skirt, bare legs, and a fuzzy old pair of pink slippers. Still, my jumbled feelings wouldn't allow me full pleasure of the view. We sat together on her sofa and remained awkwardly quiet for a long moment.

"This was a horrible day," she said. "I can't stand what's going on. No one at City Hall can." She squeezed my hand.

"This has been one of the worst days of my life," I said.

Turning toward me, she grabbed my arm with her other hand and lightly leaned her head against my shoulder. "I tried calling your cell phone a couple of times, but I didn't leave a message. I didn't want to bother you."

"I got unexpectedly busy." I told her about my interviews with Chief Rhodes and Detective Tandy. "The chief let me know roundabout that Marilyn's office computer monitor had been taken – stolen – before the police had searched the room. He didn't elaborate, but I know they're working their asses off to figure it out.

"And, get ready for this – Councilman Artic is being looked at for L.C.'s murder."

She sat up stiffly. "What? How can that be?"

"Some people, especially the police, have always believed he was into drugs, because of, you know, Kim. They apparently think something let to a shootout, or something along those lines."

"They've always thought that, no matter that they had no proof."

"In reality, we can never be sure what they've got, on anybody. But often they have no proof and simply accept their own cynicism as reality."

"They don't care what's true?"

"When you don't know for sure, it's hard not to simply believe what you figure out, and go with that. They'll have to work hard if they're going to tag Artic with murder – or drug involvement, or whatever."

"Mayor McCord, and now Councilman Artic? Murderers? This is a nightmare."

After a pause, I said, "I went to the prison to see Four Dead again. One last kick at the cat, as they say."

I caught her up with the magazine photo and ninja angle – although I mentioned no suspect names – and the witness to Four Dead's shooting. I said I'd had no idea how it connected to the City Hall mess, which, of course, wasn't altogether true. Her eyes went blank while I talked – she didn't seem to clearly comprehend. She was on overload, as were a lot of people in city government and the legal system. Me included.

I felt so comfortable with her. She seemed like a trusted squad partner. I chuckled. That was the highest praise I could give anyone.

She leaned her head against my chest. "What are you thinking?"

"Just – just how everything has happened. So quickly. So unexpectedly. Bad stuff –," I turned to look her in the eye – "and good stuff, too."

She moved up and kissed me full on the lips – a long, passionate kiss. Heat quickly spiked within, but got stuck at simmer and started dropping. Every time I felt something nice, thoughts of L.C. came to mind, and I grew cold. At least I'd become dry-eyed. In fact, my tear ducts had been overworked, and felt as though they'd been bled to dust.

Juanita moved closer and we sat for a long, silent time with our arms loosely wrapped around one another.

"What about Marilyn's office?" I asked. "Whoever took the

computer monitor must have thought you can store information on it. Must have hoped they'd find something damaging."

She once again leaned her head on my chest. "What are you looking for?"

"Some evidence that she'd put information on a computer. I'm not sure what that would be. Maybe there's a floppy or a CD laying around somewhere."

"I'll check it out."

"Tomorrow."

"Tomorrow."

CHAPTER NINETEEN

We sat for another quiet spell on her sofa, and then slipped into tender kissing. For me, the kissing initially was more comforting than sexual. Her face grew warmer and a shade darker. She touched my face, and I sensed that my skin had grown warm, also. We snuggled, and she again brought her feet up to fold them tightly under her legs, while burrowing farther into me. I held her with both arms.

"Jack," she said at last. "I know you and L.C. were great friends. You loved each other. How did you get so close?"

I drew a breath. "Well," I began, and suddenly stopped. I felt suffocated, as though shovels full of dirt were being thrown and tamped onto my face, into my mouth. As though I were being covered in a grave along with L.C. I jerked forward to catch my breath.

"What's wrong?" she asked, sitting up and placing an arm around my shoulder.

I breathed heavily, rapidly. "I'm all right." Sweat droplets stood on my skin. "I've been avoiding thoughts of L.C. as much as possible. It just took me off guard."

"We don't have to talk about it."

I nodded and sat back. She snuggled under my arm again. "L.C. and me were more than brothers," I said impulsively. Speaking of him had brought some unexpected relief. "Sounds hokey, but there was almost something spiritual about our friendship. Anyway, a couple decades ago L.C. was a shadowy criminal figure in the inner city. That was long before I knew him personally. All cops knew of him, but no one ever busted him. He was like a Mafia godfather – the head of an organization, but never in the middle of the shit."

"That takes talent."

"You bet it does. Anyway, I quit the police force and opened my own detective agency, and he left my mind. Years later, I'd heard that he'd become prominent as a layman in some church, that he'd cleaned up his act. I wondered what the scam was. Not long afterward he was arrested and convicted for murder. Received a life sentence, to be served at the state penitentiary. I followed it in the papers, but it was nothing personal to me."

Juanita gradually sat up while I talked, looking at me with deep interest.

"One day I got a letter from him. He was serving his sentence and claimed he was innocent – claimed he could prove it. He'd contacted me because I was the only ex-cop he'd heard of in the PI business, and figured I'd be the best choice to handle a criminal case. That's not true, but I didn't argue with him."

"Smart," Juanita said.

"I made an exception from my usual work with attorneys' appeals cases and insurance companies, and went to see him. He told me his story. I believed him. I took his case, but figured it was a Humpty Dumpty."

"Humpty Dumpty?"

"You know, all the pieces were there, but they couldn't be put together."

She arched her brow, in a sad-looking, puppy-dog way. "But you worked on it anyway."

"I'd never seen anyone so depressed and defeated," I said. "Yet he didn't seem bitter." I shrugged. "He'd found God, and I guess he was too beaten. He first said he wanted the truth to be known because the real killer was still out there. That's what hooked me. Then he explained his story. Everyone in prison says they're innocent, but only rarely does anyone offer good reasons as to why. That's because they can't. L.C. did, and it had more than the ring of truth. I knew it *was* the truth."

I'd warmed to telling the story.

"So, what happened?" she asked.

"I followed his leads, solved the case, and got him out of prison."

She tapped me lightly on the arm. "You know that's not what I mean." She made a slight smile.

I managed to smile back. "I know. I didn't want to bore you with the details." Actually, thinking about solving the case and the joy of helping free an innocent man, had brought a sting of regret. The thing giving way within me was giving way even more. My only way of controlling it would be avoidance.

"So, tell me," she said. "Tell me the whole story."

It was too late. The rest of the tale slipped from me the way a building topples after being ravaged by a fire. "Before his arrest for murder, L.C. really had backed away from crime. His teen-aged daughter was raped and killed by dope fiends. It broke him. But the brothers – his old acquaintances – well, they felt he had unfinished business in the street. Like, they wanted him back with their 'organization,' and were disappointed when he declined their invitations."

"You put that last part nicely."

"One learns how to translate into better language. You know?"

"Actually, I do."

"There were bitter feelings over what they believed he still owed to the – to the 'life,' so, to make a long story short, they framed him for murder. Used a handgun that had belonged to him at one time to shoot the pastor of his church, and planted some evidence in his car. They made sure he had no alibi, and got someone to play eyewitness. It was too pat, the cops and D.A. were skeptical, but as I said, L.C. had no alibi. There was enough evidence to prosecute, so the D.A. charged him. And those gangsters were ruthless. Especially the one playing 'eyewitness,' who stuck by his lie at the trial, and the jury accepted it.

"The case being old by the time I got involved actually helped me break it. The eyewitness had himself been shot a year after the trial was over, and nearly died. He's dead now, but he'd been in a wheel chair, had a colostomy bag, and was in a home receiving critical care. By the time I talked to him a few years after his own shooting, he was at hell's gate and ready to repent. He told the truth."

"Humpty didn't dumpty, this time," she said.

I smiled and kissed her cheek. "We were able to put him back together."

"We? Sounds like you did."

"From that point I gave it to the police who picked up the real shooter, and did all the rest. It was a headline case in the newspaper, and the police chief at the time made sure I got plenty of credit. My business took off. I even had a secretary for a while and hired some extra help, from time to time."

"And a great friendship between you and L.C. was forged."

"Exactly. I'd visited and stayed in touch with him while he was still locked up dozens of times before it was over. We connected in a way that L.C. called 'two bodies, one mind.' I'd never experienced that with anyone before. Certainly not my ex-wife, God bless her. Jerry Rhodes and I had something like it, but it was strictly business. With L.C., it was everything. We talked on the phone nearly every day after he got out."

My lower jaw quivered. I bit my lower lip. The tear ducts I'd given up for dead sprang back to life, and tears began welling. I turned my head and tried to sneak a hand up to wipe at them.

Juanita leaned on me, grabbed my arm and pulled my hand away. "It's okay, Jack. I understand."

Turning toward her, I tried to speak, but words would not come. My jaw and face trembled even more. More tears welled. With my last bit of determination gone, I began to cry. Tears exploded from my eyes. I tried, but couldn't stop. My lungs seized, I couldn't breathe. I began sobbing uncontrollably. I hadn't cried that hard since I was a child.

Juanita pulled me toward her. I slipped off the sofa to my knees and buried my face in her lap. I continued crying, sobbing harder and deeper and longer than I could ever remember. I cried my heart and soul out for L.C. Veasley, the gentle giant who'd defeated evil to become a great man and true community leader. I'd miss him terribly for the rest of my life.

Juanita gently ran her fingers through my hair and softly whispered that it was all right, that she'd be there for me whenever I needed her. I sobbed even harder, crying loudly in a pained voice that

I couldn't recognize as my own. Then I felt shame, for I realized I was no longer crying for L.C.

I was crying for myself.

Later, we sipped some wine, and then went upstairs. My tear ducts felt ruined once again, my face felt like a broken blister. Juanita had become remarkably calm and in control. I needed her to take control of me as well, and she steered me down the hall toward her bedroom. She left me sitting on her bed in the dark bedroom for a moment, then returned and switched on a small light on a nightstand next to her bed. She was wearing a silky white, floor-length nightgown. I stood.

"The sleeping arrangements," I said. "I'm not sure . . ."

"You have your choice. Sleep on top of my dresser, or next to me in my bed."

I almost voiced a noble-but-phony opposition to entering her bed. Being exhausted and a little tipsy from the wine, I could barely stand. Juanita unabashedly helped me undress to my underwear, and drew the blankets aside.

"Hop in," she said, guiding me to the edge of the bed. "I don't bite."

I lay down near the edge of the mattress and pulled the covers over me. She lay beside me and pulled the covers over her. I couldn't help myself. I grew aroused, alert. A thought of L.C. momentarily headed off my excitement, and then went away. The effects of the wine and being next to Juanita in her bed took over.

She came to me, kissed me lightly on the cheek and said, "Goodnight, Jack." She caressed my face. Her bare foot touched my leg. Her hand slipped to my chest, covered by my T-shirt, and innocently rubbed me in small circles.

My control flew out the window. It seemed as though all the blood in my body had flooded to my groin. I turned toward her, and she kissed me passionately, her velvety tongue dabbing at mine. Her hand moved toward the center of my body. I placed my hand on her hip, which she'd discretely made bare while getting into bed. Her skin felt hot, moist. Her hand deftly moved to the waistband of my underpants and tugged downward. I lifted my hips while she pulled.

A second later, the briefs slipped off my feet.

"I think you can handle the T-shirt," she said softly while returning her hand to my groin and gently gripping my erection.

I shuddered and quickly pulled off my T-shirt. I pulled the covers down, lifted her nightgown up and off. Our mouths locked together in a searing kiss. Our bodies pressed close, grinding together uncontrollably. She moved onto her back, baring to me her breasts, her smooth, flat stomach, and the burning place between her opening thighs. I'd never been so passionately invited to share a woman's love.

CHAPTER TWENTY

I awoke, startled, several times during the night, each time because of dreams about L.C. Juanita lay sleeping soundly next to me. Spent. I was spent, too, but my frayed nerves had prevented the deep, blissful sleep one normally has after intense lovemaking. I drifted off one last time and was awakened by Juanita's alarm clock. She sat up instantly, as though she'd been wide-awake.

"Good morning," she said, after seeing that I was awake. Her face flushed. She leaned over and kissed me warmly on the cheek.

"Good morning," I said back.

She got up, grabbed an armful of clothing from her closet, and then went into the hallway to the bathroom. I lay back, and what seemed like only moments later, she returned to the bedroom – showered, dressed, her makeup on.

"I didn't sleep real sound, you know, 'cuz of L.C.," I said while dressing.

"I understand."

"I'm going to go home and clean up."

We walked downstairs together.

"I've got a meeting this morning," she said while we left her house. "But I'll go into Marilyn's office after that. I'll call you when I can."

We kissed lightly and brushed hands before we parted. I drove home, lay on my bed, and stared at the ceiling. My night with Juanita had been overwhelming, and I was still absorbing it, and all its implications. I thought about the ninja suit in the photo, and of Four Dead. Quasi-military entities – such as law enforcement agencies – have ready access to such equipment. Tac Squad officers use that stuff. I didn't want to chase it just then – I'd get impatient and make urgent phone calls and screw things up.

I kicked off my shoes and repositioned myself on the bed. It seemed as though I'd sunk into an unripe poppy field. My eyes closed, and my body seemed to dissolve with only my thoughts remaining. The previous day's despair and the evening's ecstasy, accompanied by fitful sleep, had finally caught up with me. The last of my thoughts waved good-bye and disappeared. I heard the unmistakable sound of sleep-breathing rattle in my own throat and then I heard nothing.

I sat barely awake on the edge of my bed, clutching my cell phone. The phone's ringing on the nightstand next to me had only startled me a little, but it did the job. After answering it, Juanita said, "Hello, how are you?" in a sweet voice while I swung my feet to the floor.

"Are you going to answer me?" she asked in a singsong voice.

I thought I had. "I'm good," I said in a crusty voice.

"My meeting's been more of a wake for Marilyn. We're in the big conference room, with food and everything. People are here from all over city government to commiserate. Some business leaders, too. Marilyn's sister showed up and thanked everyone for their support. I'll get into Marilyn's office soon. Okay?"

"Yeah." I cleared my throat. "This sister that showed up today is the same sister you tried calling to get into Marilyn's house, if memory serves me."

Juanita made a small laugh. "You remembered, one whole day later. Good. Anyway, she's a wonderful gal, a lot like Marilyn." In a sex kitten voice, she whispered, "I loved last night."

Ordinarily, her sweet talk would have aroused me. "Me, too," I said thickly. I yawned. Fatigue had its hooks in me, yanking me back to the bed. Sleep. No matter what, I needed more sleep. After a lengthy pause, I said, "I gotta go. Got lots to do."

"Okay," she whispered, and hung up.

I stared at the phone for a long moment. Had I really just spoken with Juanita? It almost seemed like a dream. She'd mentioned last night – Christ, I hadn't blown her off, had I? My body launched a dose of adrenaline that misfired in a cloud of exhaustion. I lay back down, my eyes closing before my head hit the pillow. A silent black wave broke over me. I slipped into a death-like sleep.

I awoke abruptly. L.C.'s murder, again. Sometimes when I sink too deeply into sleep, a subconscious trapdoor springs open and drops me into that nightmare. The depression and anxiety I felt over his death barged through me like a thief stealing everything I owned. My adrenals had come fully awake, squirting an overdose of nervous energy through me.

My mind cleared quickly when I stood and shook myself. My mouth wasn't so easy – I almost needed a blowtorch to sear away the morning crud. While making coffee in the kitchen, I looked at the wall clock – 10:45. I remembered speaking with Juanita earlier on the phone.

My first sip of coffee twisted my knotted stomach even more tightly. I dumped the coffee in the sink. My hands shook. My wobbling knees threatened to drop me like a flunked-out college kid. I quickly pulled a chair away from the kitchen table and sat down. Murder. Mystery. Sex. My life had become a pulp fiction novel.

Within minutes I felt better and called Detective Tandy. I'd hoped he'd been given the word to help me out.

He wasn't in, and the clerk said, "He can't take your calls. He said you should call the other number you've been given."

I hung up and scrambled from my chair to the bedroom and found on the floor the shirt I'd worn the previous day. I took out the card Chief Rhodes had stuffed into the pocket. The front of the card had the crossed off name of some Deputy Chief, and on the back was hand written:

Call any time J
555-4548

I went back to my seat in the kitchen, hesitating before calling the number on the card. My questions would require legwork for answers. A police chief's legs don't do that kind of work. Drawing a deep breath, I made the call.

"Yeah," Chief Rhodes said after answering on the first ring.

"Hi, Jerry. It's—"

"Hi, Jack. I don't want to talk too long, so just listen. We checked everywhere for Roniece and couldn't find her. Our guys are talking to Hayward Artic, and he's denying everything. He's got no alibi – says he'd gone home early from the office yesterday and stayed there." I could hear car traffic in the background.

Roniece still being missing concerned me, but I kept it to myself. "Think Artic did it?"

"Don't know."

I told him about my latest interview with Four Dead, and what I'd learned about Ray-Ray. "I tried to tell Will Tandy about it but was told that only the police chief was available."

"These are strange times. But believe me, this Ray-Ray character will be checked out."

"I never had a police chief for an assistant before."

"That's an interesting point of view."

"How about the mayor?" I quickly asked. "How's that going?"

He went right along. "We have some evidence, but the D.A. says McCord's got some evidence of his own. He isn't saying what it is. McCord's attorney is shrewd as hell."

"What's the evidence you guys have?" I asked.

"No can do, my man."

"For someone who wants me to . . ."

"I want you to cooperate – do this my way."

"Okay. You're in charge. But who am I dancin' with?"

"What do you mean?"

"Like, I'm cooperating, so who's cooperating with me?"

"Me. You're dancin' and cooperatin' with me."

He really was going to be my personal police contact. All the heat must have set the kitchen afire.

I went with the flow. "Okay, then here's our first waltz. Tell me, do coppers get to keep any equipment issued them after they leave a special assignment?"

"Hell, no. The people replacing them need it. Why do you ask?"

"A hunch. What about those neat, heavy-duty vinyl jackets they let us keep when we worked together in the Tac Squad? I know that was a lot of years ago, but . . ."

"That shit we kept, yeah. But we'd paid for it ourselves. Remember? The city didn't foot the bill for stuff like that back then."

"That's right," I said. "How do they do it these days?"

"Officers can keep personal garments issued them without reimbursing the city."

"Like jackets, jumpsuits, hats, ninja suits. That stuff?"

"Yeah."

I suppressed my discomfort and kept grilling the good chief.

"There's a guy who got shot and killed two years ago who I think was a snitch for the Narcotics Squad. I'd like to know who worked him, and if the dude did any good." I cringed. Asking a police chief for that kind of inside information was like asking someone to cure cancer.

"Done. Give me his name."

Shocked, I gave him Jamal McKee's name.

"Anything else?" he asked, as crisp and politely as a chauffeur asking a dignitary his next destination.

"Lots. But some things I still want to keep under my hat."

"I trust you, Jack. That's why I'm doing this. Anything else you want to know?"

I lunged again at the jugular. "When can you tell me about the mayor's case? Not knowing if he's dirty is holding me back."

"That involves the D.A. I just can't say at this time."

"Right. We have to accept our handicaps and hope for the best." I was working him as though he were some scruff from the streets. It made me sick – he knew exactly what I was doing.

"Everything takes time, Jack. You know me. I use models to help me construct theories about crimes. I have to think it through, and like I said, that takes time."

What the hell was he talking about? "That sounds good, Jerry. Whatever it takes."

"I just had a thought," he said. "Suppose a guy is a circumstantial suspect only in a crime. But he's the logical suspect, and investigators believe he did it. So they talk to him, and the D.A. reviews the matter, and it's razor thin on whether he's charged with a crime or not. Follow me so far?"

"Oh, yeah." I'd always loved Jerry's obvious analogies.

"But after a few days, the suspect's lawyer calls the D.A. and says his client has information that can help prove his innocence. He wants a meeting with the D.A. and the cops. Looks like there could be trouble, from a prosecutorial standpoint. Right?"

"Could be. But it's also good if the suspect really didn't do it. I mean, you want the truth. Right?"

"It's good when an innocent person is proven so. Other things aren't good. For instance, if it's a highly political incident, and the news coverage has been exploding everywhere, *and you don't have another suspect* . . . Still follow?"

"But no one's been cleared, yet. Hypothetically, I mean. Right?"

He hesitated. "No. In my hypothetical, it hasn't come to that. But if it does, politics trumps. The focus shifts away from the crime. And you know to whom it would shift, don't you?"

I certainly did. "Do you have any other hypotheticals, Jerry?"

"I got a million of 'em. There's another intriguing one that I'm not ready to get into, yet."

"There's no good model to use for solving that one, I take it?"

"It's on the tough pile, yeah. But I do have some thoughts."

"Oh, come on. Let's play Clue."

"Let's say a witness saw an eventual murder victim going into the eventual suspect's work place, just before the killing."

"Did anyone see either of them inside the workplace?"

"Workin' on it."

"Did any one see either of them leave?

"In progress."

"From there, we know the victim and his – or her – car ended up in an alley where he – or she – was killed. Right?"

"Right."

I laughed. "I'm wondering how closely this model comes to L.C.'s murder."

"You don't have a fishing license, brother," he said. "But I will say that there exists other pieces yet to be inserted into the construct I've just given you."

Sometimes Jerry's over-articulation was annoying. "So, anyone speculating on that would just have to wait until names, and places, and stuff like that became available. You know, work with what they've got. Which is nothin.' Right?"

"Yes."

"Are miracles part of your construct?"

"Christ, I hope so."

CHAPTER TWENTY-ONE

We rang off. Lacking needed information from the chief had me on ice, but I didn't have to be completely immobile. Since I was going to play *real* detective, I decided to start by checking out the scene of L.C.'s shooting. Being a fresh investigation, the crime scene would certainly still be closed off, but I wanted to see it, even if from afar. I wanted to *feel* it.

I drove through the inner city, taking the city streets rather than the freeway. It was almost noon, the sun shining and the day hot and muggy. A yellow haze seemed to hover all around, dimming the sun's light. There weren't many people on the streets. I saw them anyway, in my mind's eye, exclusively black people, walking and weaving their way in and out of the streets and sidewalks, the way they had when I'd patrolled the same streets in a police squad car.

The neighborhood's depressed atmosphere hung more oppressively than weather conditions ever could. I told myself I only felt it because I knew it was there. I arrived at the alley between Currie and Founder streets, where L.C. had been killed. Two police cruisers were parked at the entrance of the alley, which divided the block lengthwise. I drove past slowly. About 50 feet into the alley a uniformed and a plainclothes officer stood, talking.

Ubiquitous yellow police tape bounded the area, wrapped around telephone poles, garbage cans, and a couple of garages. On one garage apron, parked slightly askew, was L.C.'s car. The driver's side door stood slightly open. A jolt went through me at the sight. I couldn't help but imagine the moment when L.C.'s body had been removed from the car.

The neighborhood was another one of those End-of-the-Earth places, with each block having more empty lots than houses. No one really lived there, they existed, mostly to sell and use dope. The area was numb. Dead. The sounds of gunshots were common – any time of day, every day. It seemed as though a full-scale military skirmish could take place without anyone caring enough to call the police.

There was nothing to achieve there, so I checked the one clue Jerry had given me and drove to City Hall, backtracking the most likely route L.C. had taken from there to the alley. I still couldn't understand why L.C. drove to that spot. After a block I noticed two separate sets of tire skid marks, one behind the other. Each set stretched 15 to 20 feet. After another block, more double skid marks, about the same length, and this time next to each other. Several more dual patches of black laid rubber appeared on the street, all the way back to City Hall.

A short skid mark lay just outside the garage entrance to City Hall. I noted the location of all the marks, then drove back to the crime scene the way I'd come. The skid patch trail looked like a start-stop car chase to me. The trail could be something pointing to Hayward Artic – maybe L.C. learned something about the councilman's activities and went to City Hall to threaten him, and Artic followed him in his car and caught him at Currie and Founder. Maybe someone else had chased L.C. – someone with penchant for using ninja suits from time to time. Perhaps the police had already seen the skid marks. I'd check with the chief.

While parked near the alley and finishing my notes, my cell phone rang. It was Juanita.

"Hi," I said, glancing at my wristwatch. 12:10. "Did your meeting end?"

"Yes, about an hour ago. I checked Marilyn's office, but found nothing important."

"That figures. How's her sister doing?"

"Okay, I guess. She's pretty tough. I talked to her for a long time during the meeting. She held her composure. I mentioned that the police had searched Marilyn's house and office for clues. She'd known about both, and the burglary at Marilyn's, and said she'd already gone through the house herself. Her eyes were finally getting red and moist, and she left."

"Anything else?"

"I told her the City government wanted to recover any business information Marilyn may have had on her computer. Or computer disks, and if Marilyn had kept any of that stuff at her house. By the way, Marilyn's laptop computer is missing from her house, in case the police don't know."

"Did I ask if you have your PI license?"

"Remind me never to get one."

"Smart woman."

"Is there any news about Roniece?"

"She's still in the wind. The cops checked the North 14th Street address I gave them and she wasn't there. I'm not surprised – she has to know about L.C.'s death, and plans on staying out of sight. Anyway, the cops have the place planted, in case she shows up."

"Do you think she's okay?"

"I've got my doubts. I'm going to see if I can wriggle some bait and find out."

"The police are involved. Won't they . . . ?"

"I'll approach on tiptoe."

She sighed. "How will anyone figure out who did these murders?"

"Like I've said, I don't think the mayor killed Marilyn. But I have to admit that he *could* have. As far as L.C.'s murder – who knows? Both killings are still considered whodunits. That means figure out motives first."

"How'll you proceed?"

"I'm gonna make my next move. Then I'm going to make some phone calls and check out some stuff."

"That's clear as mud. What's your next move? What are you going to do?"

"At the risk of sounding mysterious and being annoying, I'd rather not say at this time."

"Just be careful."

If I were really going to be careful, I'd go home and stay there, and not make my next move. "Don't worry." We hung up.

My car tires squealed when I pulled away from the curb. I looked up Colette's phone number and called her, all the while driving fast and straight to my apartment.

"This is Mina," Colette's voice said on her answering machine after a few rings. "Leave a message. Hope to see you soon." She spoke in an embarrassingly phony, sexy voice. Soft music played in the background.

After the beep, I told her to call me as soon as possible, and continued barreling toward my house.

"First things first," I said out loud after parking my car and trotting to my apartment, to my bedroom, to the lowest drawer of my dresser. I dug through clothing to the drawer's bottom and pulled out my Glock 10, Model 22 .40-caliber pistol. I glanced at the semi-automatic gun's dull black metal finish and black, space age plastic frame and grips. With a 16-shot capacity, it was a wicked piece. A rapid-fire trigger mechanism made it the next best thing to a machine pistol.

The magazine was fully loaded. The chamber contained a round. I shoved the gun into a holster and tucked it in the waistband at the small of my back, and pulled my shirt over it. Of course, choosing to arm myself meant I could end up in a gunfight. Oddly, that prospect never frightened me when I was a cop, but it terrified me at that moment. Being in a shoot-'em-up would be different than before. This time, I'd be without police backup, without the color of authority.

I grabbed two more loaded clips from the drawer, stood, and quickly left my house. After checking a few details, I'd go check in with Juanita at City Hall. L.C.'s killer could be there, and might resent me showing up. If things went wrong after I got there, my Glock could get a workout. A queasy feeling had me thinking they could be installing metal detectors after that day. For a moment, I sat in my car in the garage, trying to clear my mind.

It was time to let my instincts have full input. That's hard to do when you're a private citizen sticking your nose into a murder investigation. I started by consciously admitting something I'd strongly considered but avoided almost since the beginning – whoever killed Marilyn Chase worked at City Hall, and I wasn't thinking of Mayor McCord. That person also killed L.C. Veasley, and all of it had something to do with Roniece Veasley and drugs.

I continued thinking that Roniece's initial disappearance from the Summerfest grounds was critical. She'd run from someone. But who could it have been? Roniece wasn't talking, and no one seemed to know whether anyone else from City Hall had been there that day.

Hayward Artic could certainly fit as a suspect for L.C.'s murder. If he really were involved with drugs, and L.C. had somehow found that out or been led to another wrongdoing, and had gone to City Hall to confront him about it, Artic would have had a strong motive to act. The only other people at City Hall I had dealt with were Juanita and, of course, little Vinny Dragos.

Vincent Dragos. He'd been on my mind since I saw the ninja photo in the gun magazine. There wasn't enough to make any hard connections – certainly, there was no known motive.

The one thing I needed was Roniece's cooperation, if she were still alive. I was certain she knew enough to blaze a trail to Marilyn and L.C.'s killers. Knowing who she'd run from at the Summerfest grounds would be important. Roniece could potentially have information that linked to all things.

I started the engine and drove off. If I didn't hear from Colette soon, I'd go to City Hall and see Juanita. I decided I'd camp out there, somewhere in the building, at least.

I called Chief Rhodes back.

"Yeah, Jack," he said.

"Pretty sure of yourself."

"You're the only one who has this number."

I again heard street sound in the background. "Where are you?"

"On the street, in regular clothes."

It felt as though he knew something about the investigations that he hadn't yet mentioned, which would make sense.

"Okay. Do Tac Squad officers still get ninja suits?" I asked.

"Yeah. They have for years. Why?"

"I'll tell you when I think it's right," I said, without irony.

He didn't skip a beat. He gave me a cell phone number to call and said, "Mention your name when the man answers. He's from the Narcotics Squad. He'll give you what you need on Jamal McKee."

I didn't skip a beat. "I'm gonna make that call, now."

CHAPTER TWENTY-TWO

I called the cell number and spoke with a gruff officer who did not identify himself. He sounded like someone of higher rank who'd been given a shit job and didn't like it.

"This is Jack Blanchard. Chief Rhodes gave me—"

"I know who the hell had you call," he said snappily. "Let's get on with it."

I pulled to the roadside and furiously wrote notes while he nonchalantly recited his first piece of information. . . .

Detective Vince Dragos had used Jamal McKee as an informant when he worked on the Narcotics Squad.

The words rammed into me with the force of a dozen jackhammers. I swelled with excitement.

The pissed-off cop continued speaking in a droning voice, reluctantly telling me more details. McKee had helped Dragos make a few small to medium sized drug pinches, then one big one.

A John Doe investigation was held afterward and 11 people were indicted for drug dealing, including two as "drug kingpins." Dragos got a lot of praise and publicity, and McKee got a suspended sentence on his own charges. Sometime later, Dragos was transferred to the mayor's office. That was all he had.

"Thank you," I said. "That'll—"

"Yeah," the officer said, and hung up.

I paused to collect my thoughts. Dragos had made a big pinch, all right. And publicly he'd become a fair-haired boy, even if some police department insiders still held him in low esteem. Any mayor would love having a celebrated guy like that at his side, and Dragos was slick enough to play the role of humble hero. He was slick enough to play a lot of things.

I was ready to directly acknowledge my ninja photo hunch – Four Dead had ID'd it as the same type worn by the Jones gang killer. Tac Squad officers use ninja suits during special operations. Vince Dragos had been a Tac Squad officer and subsequently a narcotics dick. He'd have certainly kept his ninja suit from his Tac Squad days. All cops did.

His image jumped into my mind. I was on the verge of accusing a police detective of shooting Earl Jones and company – accusing Dragos of being a mass murderer. I'd have to have my dominoes set right in order to push that one.

But I had to deal with my current lack of information – of proof. However weak the link, Dragos was associated through Jamal McKee to Four Dead – and thereby to Earl Jones. And to Roniece Veasley, at least by implication. By this time I couldn't believe that Dragos *hadn't* himself been involved with drugs. With Jones, Roniece, possibly even Four Dead. If *that's* what Marilyn Chase thought she knew . . .

But based on what I had, I couldn't unlock the door. The time wasn't yet right even for an implication.

A mosaic of the whole drama appeared in my mind. McCord and Artic were vaguely set in the center. Next to them Detective Dragos's image solidified and grew, as though he'd taken possession of the ring. Roniece was next to him, and Four Dead was beside her. Juanita, Chief Rhodes, and I were surrounding all of them, staring blankly, looking in different directions. The murder victims, from Earl Jones and his companions, to Marilyn Chase, to L.C. Veasley, littered the outer edges. I felt the way Four Dead must've felt, with my own portrait of murder filling my head.

Distressingly, the picture remained fluid. I wanted McCord and Artic to be gone. I wanted the killer in a bull's eye in the center. I *didn't* want to see anyone added to those who were already dead.

I thought about Roniece. She'd always gone to Colette's for refuge. I could think of only two reasons why she hadn't been there when the cops checked there that morning – she'd gone deeper into the streets, or she was dead. I strongly feared the latter, and Vince Dragos's image grew even larger in my mind.

I shook my head. It was all too fantastic.

I realized I'd remained parked while daydreaming, and looked around the neighborhood. Across the street an older black man was watering his front lawn, glancing at me with a suspicious look. A woman, probably his wife, disappeared through the lower front door of a two-story bungalow on the property. She was probably calling the cops. No stranger just pulled over on those streets unless they were up to no good. I drove away.

Driving and waiting were all I could do, a maddening proposition, for I knew that things were happening fast.

A short while later my phone rang.

"Is this Jack?" The husky-yet-pleasant voice was that of Colette.

"I'm glad you called back," I said, as casually as possible.

"I'm scared for Roniece," she said quickly.

Once again, I pulled to a street curb. A swab of anxiety blotted moisture from my mouth and throat. My heart pounded fast and arrhythmically, seemingly beyond its physical limits.

"What is it?" I managed to ask.

"She came over yesterday. In the afternoon. She didn't say nothin', but she was scared. She went right upstairs. Later I heard her yelling – I think she was on a cell phone. I couldn't hear what she said."

"Where is she? I need to speak with her."

"She's gone. The cops come over this morning and I let them check upstairs. Don't know where she went. It look like she left in a hurry."

"Maybe she headed for the hills."

"She never split like that without tellin' me. Never. After the cops left I got a call from a neighbor sayin' a unmarked squad car was parked. The dudes in it were lookin' at my house."

The cops certainly knew things that I hadn't been told. Things I *needed* to know, if I was going to help. Damn it, Jerry Rhodes. I never eat half a sandwich.

"Do me a favor, Colette. Call me back if you hear from Roniece, all right?"

I hung up and looked around. This time I'd parked on a block with no houses, only stretches of vacant lots looking like post-apocalyptic prairies on either side of the street, overgrown in places with tall grass and weeds, littered with debris. A rat scurried to the sidewalk from beneath a large moldy cardboard box. Sensing its sudden vulnerability, it quickly dashed back to the safety of the garbage pile. At least the rat wouldn't call the cops on me.

I called Jerry Rhodes.

"Yeah, Jack," he said, after the first ring.

"It's me, Jack," I said sarcastically.

"What's up?"

I told him about Roniece having been at Colette's house, but mysteriously leaving sometime overnight. Whatever was going on, I was certain she wouldn't be returning.

"Damn," the chief said. "She knows something. We gotta find her."

"Colette thinks Roniece is in trouble. Says she would never leave like this without telling her."

"We'll keep looking. What else can we do? Is there anything else?"

After mentioning Vince Dragos's use of an informer linked to Earl Jones and Kim Artic, and Dragos's big drug bust behind it, the chief grew silent. I didn't tell him what I believed – I wanted him to draw his own conclusions.

"And you know," I said, "Roniece Veasley was involved with Jones and Kim, and started working at City Hall just before Marilyn Chase was killed, and now L.C. Veasley is . . . You know where I'm goin'."

More silence.

"And, of course, Roniece is L.C.'s sister, and Hayward Artic is your suspect in his killing."

I infused my tone with irony, whether he caught it or not. Vince Dragos's name reverberated inside my head.

"If Dragos is working today," the chief said, "he'd have known about Veasley's murder first thing this morning. With all he knew about those people, it would be standard for him to call Homicide – especially in a big deal like this. I'd have heard if he'd called, or at least if someone from Homicide had called and left a message. He may have an 'aw shit' coming."

I understood better than most why just one "aw shit" can wipe out all "atta boys." The chief had a keen rat smeller – he'd know if anything were amiss.

After I explained about the tire skid marks along the likely path taken by L.C. from City Hall, he said, "Artic has been questioned and released pending further inquiry. Told not to leave town, and all that. We had to let him go, with only the flimsiest of evidence and Artic's big shot attorney calling – well, calling the D.A. and me direct, for chrissakes. Artic's denials can't be disproved. Yet. I'll get all this to the detectives right away."

"What about Mayor McCord? Where's he?"

"In the D.A.'s office, as we speak."

"How's it going?" I didn't expect a straight answer.

"Okay for him. He's got notes and other stuff backing himself up."

"Could someone ask him if he was at the Summerfest grounds the day Roniece took off? If he was, ask how he got there."

"Sure. Got a reason?"

"Yeah. But I can't say right now."

If my dominoes were beginning to fall right, the mayor could have been there, and Dragos could have driven him there, and he and Roniece could have seen each other.

He accepted my answer without comment, and once again we ended our phone conversation. I drove to City Hall quickly – to pick Juanita's brain as much as to be with her. Her solidly logical mind made her an instinctive investigator.

I arrived at her office shortly after one o'clock. She sat at her desk, busily tapping on her computer keyboard. She turned her gaze from her computer monitor, looked at me while I entered, and made a dreary half-smile.

"Hi," she said, and turned back to the computer. On her desk blotter laid a stack of computer diskettes and CDs.

"Maybe we're in luck," she said, while pausing from her task. "Julia Chase took the hint and went to Marilyn's house straight from here, and found these in a false bottomed drawer of Marilyn's desk."

She pointed at the stack. "She brought them all right here, thinking they might be important."

I was surprised and grateful, but not enthused. I leaned over, bracing myself with my arms on Juanita's desktop so I could see the computer screen.

I said, "Odds aren't too good we'll find anything."

Juanita continued tapping at the computer keyboard. "No bad hunches. Remember?"

"Right. You're a thorough investigator."

And I was a mostly burned-out cynic, having a long history of dashed high hopes. But you can't quit until the whistle blows, and sometimes it took new talent, like Juanita, to remind me – to remind all experienced investigators.

"I've already checked a few disks. None of them are labeled, and two are blank. So far, I've found nothing relevant on those with any information at all on them." There were at least a dozen disks stacked on her desk. "I'm almost done checking. I'm still hoping."

"You've already had time to check everything?" I asked while sitting in the chair to the side of her desk. The Glock dug into my tailbone when I sat.

"I'm afraid so."

I sat back, folding my hands across my stomach. Juanita stared with hard, beetle-browed intensity at the computer screen while she furiously typed away, then manipulated the mouse, then typed some more.

My cell phone rang, and I yanked it from my belt. "Hi, Jerry," I said when I answered it.

"Yeah, how are ya'?" the chief said. "*Where* are ya'?" he asked, before I could say anything.

"City Hall. Juanita Velez's office. She's checking some records."

"Then the rumors about you and her are true. Is she comin' up with anything?"

"You knew all along they weren't rumors. And you don't even know what she's looking for. And no, not yet."

"By the way, Vince Dragos is working today, but he only called himself in from his cell phone because the mayor's, ah, indisposed."

"Well, I . . ."

"And we're checking the tire marks. Apparently some patches left groove marks. It won't make a case, but we're gonna end up at City Hall to make comparisons with the tires on some cars parked around there. Artic is supposed to have gone there after he left the D.A.'s office to meet with his attorney. You may see him."

I planned on staying out of sight.

"You thinking of speaking with Dragos?" I asked.

"Do you know why we towed the mayor's private vehicle during the initial phase of Marilyn Chase's murder investigation?"

Normally, I'd have told him to answer my question first, but this was no time for ribbing. "No."

"We found a small spot of blood in the trunk. Turned out to be Marilyn's, mixed with her saliva. By the way, she'd been strangled."

My face instantly burned so intensely with mortification a red glow circled my vision. "You're kidding. That's a slam-dunk. Why isn't he being charged?"

"That's part of what he and his lawyer are presenting to the D.A. He's got notes and other stuff showing he ain't the only one who drives the car. He leaves it during the day at the City Hall garage. The keys are available for maintenance people to jockey it around. Being his driver, Dragos uses it. Marilyn Chase even used it. And there've been others."

I dropped my hand with the phone to my lap. Dragos. Juanita looked at me. Her expression had grown from blank to curious to deep concern while listening to me talk. She leaned forward, as though she were attempting to hear the other side of the phone conversation.

I asked the chief, "How's the mayor's alibi look?"

"That's another reason we'll be at City Hall soon."

"You seem to be closing in on something, and I'm feelin' out of the loop. Why are you keeping me on board at all?"

"I've been meaning to discuss that with you. Remember, you're just a citizen, but you know the score on acting as an agent of the police. If you so act, nothing you'd tell us could be used as evidence. Remember the law, and the rules I've endorsed and enforced."

The odor of cigar smoke seemed to grow in my nostrils.

"Jack?" the chief said. "You there?"

"Yeah. I'm here."

"Call me after you're done to tell me your status."

I pushed the phone's off button. Juanita had returned to her computer and seemed to be paying extra attention to whatever was currently on the monitor.

I certainly did "know the score" on acting as an agent of the police. Without direction, I could search places and "confiscate" things, and ask people questions without legal restrictions.

Without police direction.

It was a typical example of Jerry's resourcefulness – turn loose a PI on the sly and let him help the police department with a criminal investigation.

"I've checked through all the disks, and most are blank," Juanita said, bringing me back to the moment. She kept her hard glare on the computer screen. "There's nothing obvious on the few that have anything at all. I'll re-check one that has a spreadsheet with a City Hall employees day-off schedule, going back more than two years."

"Why's that important?"

"I don't know, except that the disk was created the day Marilyn died."

My phone rang and again I snatched it from my belt.

A familiar, shaky-sounding woman's voice said, "This is Roniece."

CHAPTER TWENTY-THREE

"Roniece!" I shouted.

Juanita jerked her head sharply toward me when she heard me yell.

"Roniece, where are you? *How* are you?"

"I'm okay, but somethin's goin' down. I don' wanna talk on the phone."

She sounded strange and distant, almost as though she were reading her words.

"Where are you? I'll come get you."

After a moment, she said, "That won't work. Where you now?"

When I said I was in Juanita's office she paused again and then said she'd call back.

"You've heard about L.C., I take it?" I said before she disconnected.

"Yeah," she said blandly, "I ain't got time."

She hung up.

I'd been staring at Juanita during the conversation. She'd dropped her jaw, her eyes bugged.

"She's all right?" Juanita said.

"She's alive. She sounded strange. I don't know what to make of it."

"Well, her brother's been murdered, and with everything else going on, she's no doubt in shock."

"She sounded as though she couldn't care less." I snapped my cell phone shut and clipped it back onto my belt. "She's in charge, right now. I'll just have to wait until she's ready to call back."

Juanita continued gaping.

I readjusted myself in my seat, the gun at the small of my back still poking me.

"Let's go over the time sheet," I said.

"Yes. Absolutely." She reached toward the computer keyboard before looking and her fingers started tapping.

I got up from my chair and came around her desk to stand behind her, and looked over her shoulder. The computer screen opened an elaborate spreadsheet into view.

"This day-off schedule lists payroll numbers of City Hall employees," she said, while using the mouse to scroll through the screen. "I don't know why she felt this was important." Juanita held up a second computer disk. "She'd copied it onto another disk."

I leaned closer. "How can we tell which of those numbers she was interested in?"

"They look like employee payroll numbers, but there's no key. Let me look at the other disk."

She popped out the current disk and inserted the copied one. She quickly scrolled through the entire sheet.

"There, at the bottom," she said while pointing at the screen. "She added an employee number onto this disk – 35161-005. It's listed previously in numerical order in the main roster."

"But no idea who it belongs to, or what she was looking for. Is that right?"

"Not on the disk. I'll check the number in the city-wide system." She switched screens to one emblazoning the city's logo and typed in access codes to arrive at the city employee section. In a moment, the payroll number showed up, alongside a name. . . .

Vincent Dragos.

I straightened and folded my arms across my chest. A feeling of satisfaction whisked through me. "And the off schedule goes back, what, two years or so? That's the time of the Jones shooting. Dragos was transferred to City Hall around then." My moment of gratification began slipping. "What exactly had Marilyn connected dots to?"

Juanita turned around in her chair to look up at me. "I can't tell.

At least, not yet."

"It begins with drugs, I'm sure."

And it ended in murder, I said to myself.

She turned back to the computer and continued pitter-pattering on the keyboard and operating the mouse. I stood for a long moment, and looked away from the monitor, the rapidly flashing images meaning nothing to me.

"Do you think Dragos had anything to do with Earl Jones?" she asked while still studying the screen.

"I been thinkin' that for a while, and I just found some information that suggests it. I can't figure exactly what Marilyn was onto, but it seems like she was trying to build a case against him. Give me time."

We probably won't have it, I didn't say.

Juanita continued her work, stopping at times to squint, look puzzled, and then go on. I walked around to the front of her desk and paced impatiently, my hands stuffed in my pockets.

"We think Marilyn started all this the day Roniece ran from the festival grounds," I said. "Right?"

Juanita continued staring intently at the computer screen. "Yes."

"Could Dragos have been at the grounds, even if the mayor wasn't?"

She swung her chair back to her desk, situated her legs beneath, and looked at me. "People at City Hall have seen him at lots of functions that the mayor doesn't attend. They always suspected him of spying, among other things."

An expression of horror grew on Juanita's face. I felt the same look growing on mine. I could feel tumblers rapidly falling into place in our respective minds, lining up with the same conclusion – Dragos had been at the festival grounds that day, and Roniece had run from *him*. He had indeed been linked to Roniece's activities – drugs and who knew what else – and Marilyn had figured it out.

Then she got in his way.

"I'm gonna call the chief," I said, once again pulling the cell phone from my belt. "They gotta get Dragos in custody *now*."

"You're calling the *police* chief?"

"Yeah. I ended up connecting with him." I prepared to punch

out Jerry's cell number on the telephone touch pad. "I'll explain later."

"And I've got something to explain about this disk," she said. "You won't believe . . ."

She looked toward the door, obviously through the pebbled glass. I watched her – a look of horror returned to her face. The door handle twisted. I stepped to the side and the door slowly opened, swinging toward me and stopping perpendicular to the doorway. I remained shielded by the door, looking through the glass. The shadowy form of a person entering the room came into view. Juanita gasped. A moment later the person moved through the door and into the office.

Roniece Veasley.

She stepped to the front of Juanita's desk, while I remained to her side. I stared hard at her profile. She had the pasty complexion of the dead. Standing still, slumping slightly, she tried in vain to straighten and square her shoulders. She looked in my direction. Dark circles rimmed her bloodshot eyes. A bruise marred her left cheek. Her lower lip was swollen. Shampoo hadn't foamed in her greasy, straggly, sweaty hair for too long. Her clothes, a white T-shirt and blue jeans, were dirty and disheveled.

"You don't look too good," I said to her.

She was still looking at me. "I feel like I'm dead." She spoke in the same tired monotone she'd used on the phone. "And I think I'm gonna *be* dead. Soon."

"Shut up," a man said harshly from behind her in the hallway.

The door swung open wider, slamming into me. I stepped back. Juanita sat back sharply in her chair, eyes opened wide. My view of Roniece had again become obscured by the wide open door. An instant later an arm swung sharply downward onto Roniece's head.

The sickening *thwap* of a blunt object striking a skull sounded. Roniece crumpled to the floor.

I stepped back farther until I saw her slumped form lying on the floor before Juanita's desk. The man stepped forward and kicked Roniece hard in the back.

"Get up, bitch," he said.

I recognized the voice.

Detective Vincent Dragos.

I reached toward my back for my gun.

Dragos moved farther into the office, arm held straight out, pointing a dark colored handgun at Juanita. In the same motion he looked at me and swung the muzzle in my direction. He pointed the gun back at Juanita, who'd stuck both arms straight above her head, and kept his eyes on me. *Don't even think about it*, I imagined him saying.

I brought my hand away from my gun and continued stepping back, sitting on the chair behind me. He swung the gun around and again pointed it at me. He swayed to one side, and then righted himself.

"Private prick," he said, his voice grinding with disgust. His face flushed while he squeezed his lips together. "What the fuck you think you're doin'?"

The black hole in the muzzle of his gun was all I saw. It looked wide and deep, dark as the bottom of a grave. I raised my hands above my head. The strong odor of stomach-soured alcohol began filling the room. The stink came from Dragos, who looked as though he'd been on a daylong drinking binge. His sweat-soaked white dress shirt hung loose from his trousers, the collar open, no tie, sleeves unbuttoned. He, too, had dark rimmed, bloodshot eyes. His matted hair stuck out wildly from his head, as though he'd escaped an electric chair before the current could fry his whole body.

"Get up an' turn aroun'," he said to me. "Put your hands agains' the wall."

I did as I was told. He stepped forward and patted me down, quickly finding and snatching the Glock from my waistband.

"Nice piece," he said. "Against the law for you to be carryin', though." He stepped back. "Turn aroun' slow an' sit down."

Again, I did as I was told.

"Yer under arrest," he said, laughing. He pointed his gun at me again. "Yer Honor, the arresting officer has foun' the defen'ant guilty," he said, and made an explosion sound while jerking his gun up and over his head.

He laughed again. He was funny.

He stuck my gun in his front waistband, muzzle pointing toward his crotch – Old West style, we used to call it. "Cowboy cops" did that, and, sadly, not enough of them had experienced the Unexpected

Discharge That All Men Fear.

Roniece still lay on the floor, not moving. Juanita and I continued sitting with our hands stuck high in the air. Drunkenness and gravity conspired to pull Dragos's arm downward. Soon the gun hung by his side.

He sneered at me, his eyes wild looking. "Stupid fucker," he said, slurring his words. "Never, never, never in'erfere with the police. It'll get ya killed. Every time." He drew his arm back up and waved the gun at me.

I drew a deep breath, fearing it might be my last. He squeezed one eye closed and took deliberate aim with the gun at my head. He laughed and lowered the gun once again.

"Not here," he said. "Not now."

Behind him Roniece stirred on the floor, pushing herself up to her knees. Dragos turned his head to look at her, still unsteadily pointing the gun in my direction. Roniece moved slowly, obviously in great pain.

I knew why he was desperate, and why he'd chosen to drink himself into near oblivion, but why he'd come to City Hall in his condition, dragging along a battered Roniece Veasley, was beyond my ability to imagine.

But then, there was certainly a lot I didn't know. Maybe there had become too much for Dragos to deal with. Maybe he wasn't sure he'd come out of whatever jam he'd gotten himself into, and had thrown everything to the wind.

"Get up, and get in that chair," Dragos shouted at Roniece, who dragged herself to a chair on the other side of the room.

"Now," he said, swinging his upper torso back to face Juanita, who sat still and terrified with her hands above her head, "you an' me got some bidness."

CHAPTER TWENTY-FOUR

He leaned over the desk, nearly toppling, straining to see the computer screen. "What 'cha got there?" He squinted, then straightened and laughed. "You're gonna have to tell me."

Juanita remained frozen, unable to speak or move.

"Tell me, goddammit!" Dragos yelled, pointing his gun at her again. "I know what you're doin'. I know what *she* was doin'."

Juanita's eyes bulged. She brought her arms down while turning toward the computer keyboard. My heart pounded hard, irregular rhythms. One by one, my hunches were being confirmed.

Juanita began explaining about Dragos's payroll number to him, and that the spreadsheet went back . . .

"Two years. I know. She said she was gonna show I was involved with drugs by all the 'personal' time I took. Said she knew people who'd corroborate her story."

He still hadn't identified who "she" was, but he didn't have to. I could almost hear Marilyn Chase taunting him.

Dragos brought his hand to his forehead. He lowered the gun with his other hand. My gun poked out from his waistband, tempting me to make a move for it. I didn't. He began weeping.

"Bitch!" he said through his sobs. "Fuckin' bitch. She didn' make sense – but I couldn'..."

"Couldn't what?" I asked, my voice pinched with anxiety. I kept my hands above my head.

He dropped his hand from his brow and turned toward me.

Tears streaked his face. "Shut up. How do you know who I'm talkin' about?"

"Marilyn Chase. I've put some things together."

"You put some things together," he said, in a singsong, mocking voice. He again pointed the gun at me. "Its time for me to take some fuckin' things apart."

Suddenly, Juanita began to cry.

His eyes remained on me. "Shut up," he yelled at her.

I tried keeping his attention on me. "How long were you and Earl Jones and Roniece hooked up? After Jamal McKee introduced you, I mean?"

A look of shock and then rage moved over his face. He began trembling.

I kept the pressure on. "McKee helped himself off the hook even more by cutting you in on Jones's action, didn't he?"

He turned to face me full on.

"Jones should have been arrested on a drug kingpin charge, right? Instead, he got off scot-free and you helped him keep operating."

Bemusement gradually replaced Dragos's angry expression.

"Roniece burned you at the festival grounds, didn't she?" I said. "You thought you'd gotten away clean, and she was just a crackhead who disappeared – as credible as a cockroach, with a burned-out doper brain. She turns up like a bad penny and runs away. That meant she was on the ball enough to hurt you.

"Marilyn knew something bad was going on, and *she* threatened to burn you. She didn't *have* to know exactly what you'd done. You had to act."

"Couldn't take a chance," he said, defeated. The color drained from his doughy face. Apparently I'd figured out more than he'd suspected.

"It don' matter what you figured," Dragos said, his voice becoming a dry wheeze. "Everything will be over before you go any farther."

"How do you know how far I've gone? How do you know what proof I have, or what I've said to anyone."

He squinted while turning his head and pointing his gun in the direction of the computer. "You jus' found them disks. Bitch here still workin' on 'em when I come in. Tha's the only thing can burn me. It's bullshit, but I gotta cover it. You ain't had time to tell anyone." He paused, swayed hard against Juanita's desk, and pushed himself upright. "Things woulda happen by now."

"Bet it pissed you off when you couldn't find the disk yourself when you broke into Marilyn's house, after you strangled her," I said.

He looked back at me, his expression blank. "What'd the fuckin' cops think, a junkie crawled through her house?"

Everything was coming together. He'd killed Marilyn to shut her up. He'd rifled through her office and took her computer monitor, and then broke into her house and took her laptop. He'd also shot L.C. – probably after Roniece called L.C. and told him the whole story, and L.C. had gone to City Hall to confront him. Hayward Artic was a patsy.

Two years before, Dragos had put on his old Tac Squad ninja suit and gunned Earl Jones and his gang. They, too, had somehow gotten in his way.

But he'd been talking too freely, too nonchalantly – not caring what I knew. That was bad. At least he'd telegraphed his plans – to do away with Juanita and me. I figured Roniece to be a goner, too, judging by the way he treated her.

"Why did you come here?" I asked. "Why aren't you half way to South America?"

"I came for *these*." Without taking his eyes off me he leaned over and snapped the floppy disk out of the computer and scooped up the remaining disks and CDs from Juanita's desktop.

"These," he said triumphantly, waving the software at me, "the only chance lef' there's proof. Ain' no proof, ain' no witnesses. They ever get me, I keep my mouth shut. I skate."

He'd had serious tunnel vision to see those disks as the only way of catching him. He was drunk and delusional, but oddly, not paranoid enough. The pressure had cracked him – he simply couldn't see beyond the momentary, the petty.

"You sure you've figured everything?" I asked.

He smiled. "*Ain' no evidence, ain' no witnesses.*" He swung the gun back and forth between Juanita and me. "Wha' they know and wha' they can prove don' add up."

I wanted to keep him talking. "So, now that you have the disk, you must be satisfied. Right?"

He waved the gun around the room. "This my las' play. I live, I go to South America."

"With all the drug money you, ah, earned from Earl Jones. And likely others. And invested and grew into—"

"Fuck you." He continued smiling idiotically. He brought the gun down to his side.

I looked at Roniece, sitting bent over in her chair, clutching her arms around herself, moaning.

I pointed at her. "Why'd you bring her here? She can only be in the way."

"I answered you enough," Dragos said, turning toward me again. "S'time to go." He motioned me up from my chair with the gun.

"You need to keep her with you while you tie your loose ends. Right? But why? There's got to be more than just finding Juanita and me, and those stupid disks. There's more people to find, and she's gonna help. Right?"

He'd allowed me to talk, his expression growing blank. The booze weighed heavily within him, sapping his energy.

Juanita's phone rang.

"Don' answer it," he shouted.

You could almost see the alcohol thickening inside him.

The rings stopped after six, and then began again. We all sat silently. The rings stopped again, this time after three.

A moment later my cell phone rang. Dragos motioned me with the gun. "Toss it here."

I yanked it from my belt and tossed it to him. He caught it and smashed it on the floor with a blinding swing of his arm. The phone shattered. Moments later, the phone on Juanita's desk began ringing again. She remained still. The ringing stopped.

Dragos glanced at Juanita, then back at me. "Somebody's tryin' to get aholt of you both."

He was slurring his words more each time he spoke. He leaned and stumbled slightly while looking at me, then back at Juanita.

I shrugged. "Lot's of people call us both."

An air of clarity returned to him, unclouding his rheumy eyes, dusting his face once again with an angry, sober look. "They know yer together, an' they know yer in her office," he said, raising his voice, pointing at Juanita with the gun. His eyes widened. "Wha's goin' on?"

"You don't *know*?"

"I'm a dummy." He shakily pointed the gun back at me. "You gotta educate me."

I'd spoken too soon. My big mouth had forced my brain to dig out an answer.

"The police think Juanita may be next on the list to be killed," I said. "They know I've been working as her bodyguard."

He sneered. "I oughtta fuckin' shoot you both right now."

"Why? What other reason would I have to be with her so much?"

He drew one arm up to wipe sweat from his face onto his shirtsleeve. "Tryin' to drill 'er brains out, like everyone else." He leaned on Juanita's desktop. "You been helpin' her figure shit out." His head lowered, his stare dropped toward the floor while he spoke.

He knit his brow and narrowed his eyes. "So, the cops are comin,' huh? Time to go."

The old saw about never pushing too far a homicidal drunkard who is pointing a loaded gun at you came to mind, but I pushed, anyway. "You killed Earl Jones and the others two years ago. Didn't you? He'd crossed you, somehow. You wore your ninja suit that you'd kept from your days on the Tac Squad, and hit him in the alley after drawing him out."

He looked at me and smiled. "Your gumshoe stuck in yer brain, dick. Gummin' up the whole works." He began to laugh, a forced, uproarious belly laugh.

He turned to Roniece, still doubled over on her chair. "Wanna tell 'im who shot Jonesy an' your girlfriend, Kimmy Artic?" He paused. "Tell him," he shouted.

She didn't respond.

He stepped toward her and raised his gun above her head. "Goddammit girl, you tell him!"

She lifted her head. The pain of Dragos's battering had pinched her face into a mask of agony. She held her side – the side where he'd kicked her.

"Nobody know fo' sho'," she said hoarsely.

He brought the gun back down to his side. "Ray-Ray knows '*fo sho*,' and when we get to him, he'll say it."

She shook and lowered her head.

Ray-Ray! This was where he really fit in!

Dragos swung his arm upward and struck her face with the butt of his gun. Her head snapped backward and she brought her arms up to cover her face.

"See what I had to put up with?" he asked while turning toward Juanita and me.

What exactly did Ray-Ray have to say? I wondered where Ray-Ray had been, how he'd avoided the cops.

"Is that why you brought her?" I asked. "She's gonna help you get to Ray-Ray?"

I glanced at Roniece. The girl had been up to her eyeballs in everything.

I looked back at Dragos. "Why? He the only one left who can dime you off?"

He turned to Roniece. "Who's Ray-Ray gonna give up, darlin'?"

She didn't answer.

Dragos looked at me. "Who you think shot 'em all, super sleuth?"

Until that moment my deductions had told me it was Dragos. By his tone I thought that perhaps I'd have to re-read the deduction chapter of my private eye handbook. If I lived through this mess, that was.

I shrugged, but my mind burned rubber while I re-thought the Jones shooting scenario. I couldn't believe where my mind began taking me.

Dragos laughed.

It didn't matter where my re-scrambled deductions led me. "Forget the disks," I said. This was *my* last play – to keep him engaged until I had my chance to do . . . to do *something* – so I threw everything I had at him. "You're down cold for Marilyn Chase and L.C. Veasley."

His face reddened, his eyes narrowed. He swayed and nearly fell over. "How's that?"

My mouth worked faster than my mind. "The mayor kept his own log book of mileage on his personal car. The cops know he didn't drive it since before the night Marilyn was killed." I was winging it with the last part, but I thought there was a good chance it was true.

A fleeting, sober look cut across his face. "Tha' don' mean nothin.' Prove who the hell drove it." He reached into his pocket and brought out the computer disks. "These here 're it," he said, waving the disks around.

"How do you know she didn't make an encrypted copy and store the disk somewhere else?" Juanita abruptly asked, her voice quivering. Her arms were still stretched straight above her head – a pitiful sight.

He looked at her sidelong. "You didn' find nothin', it means nothin's there. Odds 're with me."

"You killed her and put her into the trunk of the mayor's car, then dumped her body," I said. "But you screwed up. You didn't know about the Mayor's logbook. You didn't know everything could be boiled down to you."

He slid his gaze from Juanita to me, pointed his gun at me and cocked the hammer. "Me an' Marilyn-bitch were in City Hall garage. Alone. Woulda been perfeck, if you hadn' stuck your nose in."

"You don't think the police would have figured it out?"

He sneered and grunted a short laugh. "This ain' TV or the movies. Mos' a those stupid, lazy bastards are only there for a paycheck."

Some of them were, he had me there. And even if they were all good and hard working, they damn well might not have been able to pin a charge on Dragos.

"And L.C. Veasley," I said. "The cops know you killed—"

"They don' know shit about L.C. Veasley, an' never will."

"Got that one covered, huh?"

He grinned. "Super sleuth. Too bad you're never gonna tell anyone." He straightened his arm and stuck the gun out farther and again drew a bead on me.

CHAPTER TWENTY-FIVE

After a moment, he let the hammer go forward and pulled up the gun.

"Everybody up," he said, looking around the room.

"What are you gonna do?" I asked. "March us off and kill us?"

"Come on, come on," he said while motioning me up from my chair to the door. "You goin' out firs'. Do what I tell ya,' or yer dead."

"There *is* nothing on any of these disks, you stupid fucker!" Juanita suddenly shouted while standing. Her face had grown deep red and rapidly phased into a throbbing purple mask. She folded her arms across her breasts, and continued shouting. "Shoot us right now, you low-life son of a bitch!" She shook while sobbing, but retained control. She stared fiercely at Dragos, staring down death – *daring* death – the way people are capable of when pushed beyond their limits.

"Nothin' on the disk, huh?" Dragos said matter-of-factly. "All this for nothin'."

"Nothin'," I said. "And here you are, your risky *play* getting' you nowhere, except puttin' your head in a noose. Everything's unraveling, Dragos. It's gettin' worse by the minute."

Roniece stood and screamed, "I ain't goin' nowhere, muthafucka! What you gonna do? See how far you git."

Dragos turned and started toward her, then stopped. "Ain't the way s'workin', Darlin'."

Roniece trembled while crouching and clutching her arms

around herself. "It don't matter no more."

"It matters. You wanna come out alive."

Dragos looked at me and again motioned me up with the gun. I slowly stood and walked toward the door, sticking my hands up, my back to him. I sensed him pointing his gun back and forth at Roniece and Juanita. "You two get moving," he said to them.

Through the pebbled glass in the office door I saw several dark, shadowy figures – figures of people crouching and advancing leapfrog style, crawling on their bellies as they got closer to the door. My eyes widened while the meaning sunk in. The police. The Tac Squad was there, establishing a perimeter, preparing to end things, one way or another.

I heard Juanita get up from her chair and walk to the side of her desk. Roniece had stood erect, and stood her ground. The officers outside moved ahead erratically, lying flat on the floor and against the walls.

I sensed Dragos turning his attention to me. After a brief pause he yelled, "Shit!" He'd looked past me and seen the dark figures through the door glass. He knew it was the cops, and he knew it was over. Some of the crawling shadows inched closer.

I ducked, turned and crouched low while throwing myself at Dragos's midsection. His drunkenness affected him less than I expected and he managed to smash his forearm into my face. I slipped to my knees and he staggered back. My hand went to his waist, to the gun grip of my Glock, and I snatched it from him. I ducked and rolled. Swaying, barely able to stand, Dragos fired two shots vaguely in my direction. The bullets whizzed past.

The explosions brought Roniece and Juanita's survival instincts to life. Both dropped to the floor – Juanita crouching behind her desk and Roniece, across the room, crawling away from Dragos. Dragos brought the gun back up and pointed it toward me. He was no more than ten feet away. Everything moved in slow motion.

I curled and dropped down farther. He shot toward me again, and again he missed badly. While pointing my gun at the center of his chest, I thanked God for drunken impairment, and rapid-fired three shots at him. All three struck his upper chest in a tight, fatal pattern – the "ten ring," as shooting instructors call it.

The roar and concussion of all the gunfire had split the air. His body shivered violently. Pinkish, spattering blood burst from his wounds after each bullet smashed into him. At his distance from me, he'd been a large, easy target. His face instantly took on the flattened, waxy look of a dead man.

He crumpled onto Juanita's desk, already loose-jointed and rubbery. The gun remained in his dead hand. He rolled and dropped to the floor, his head thudding morbidly when it struck. His body lay face up with one leg bent grotesquely at the knee and tucked under the buttocks. Blood stained his chest, but did not pool around the body. That requires a beating heart.

My ears rang. The after-effects of gunfire – the blue smoke and odor of gunpowder, even the concussion from the gunshots – slowly settled on the room, like a canvas tarp covering a dead body. Juanita had crawled to the side of her desk nearest me and crouched, still clamping her hands to her ears.

CHAPTER TWENTY-SIX

An instant later the office door blew open, banging against the wall, shattering the door glass. I tossed my gun away and remained on my knees, stretching both hands high above me. The police would quickly be through the door, and I would be in their gun sights.

A remote mechanical door opener lay on the hallway floor. The room was instantly filled with pandemonium. Helmeted and flak-jacketed police officers stuck a bulletproof shield into the doorway and followed behind it. While surveying the room, they wedged in twos through the door and filled the office like gouts of jellied blood pouring from a ruptured artery. Two officers stood over Dragos's body with short-barreled shotguns pointing at it.

Two other officers pointed shotguns at me and screamed, "Freeze! Keep your hands up!"

Other officers yelled, "Clear!" Paramedics pushed their way through the clog of police while the officers pointing shotguns at me approached and roughly pulled me to my feet. Their hands thumped my body hard, as though they were trained to do pat-down searches in Braille. One of the officers spotted my gun on the floor and quickly picked it up.

I watched the paramedics go to work on Dragos while the officers handcuffed me. A kneeling attendant touched his neck, looked up and shook his head. While the police lifted me off my feet and carried me toward the wall next to the door, I saw paramedics help Roniece to her feet. She was pale and puffy-faced, unable to stand without help. Police officers immediately swarmed her and the paramedics.

The two officers put me down and pushed me hard, shoving my chest and jaw into the wall, as though they'd meant to make an imprint. The air crushed out of my lungs. One of the officers leaned forcefully with his arm on my back.

"Hello, Chief," another officer said.

All talking stopped. Police radios squawked intermittently.

"Carry on," the chief said.

Feet shuffled on the floor. Quiet conversations began.

"Who's this?" the chief said while he stood behind me.

I still hadn't seen him.

The officers spun me around and showed me to the chief, the way a young boy shows his father an athletic trophy. The chief was dressed in plainclothes . . . a white short-sleeved sport shirt and dark, casual slacks.

"We haven't ID'd him yet, sir," one of the officers said sharply. "We believe he's the man who did the shooting." The same officer had recovered my gun and held it up for the chief's inspection. The chief didn't look at it.

The chief stared at me hard in the eyes the whole time, his face expressionless. His boys and girls had handled me like a murder suspect, in spite of what they may have been told about me before the shit storm erupted. I myself was glad – they'd done their jobs properly.

"Do we need him in here?" the chief asked.

"No, sir," an officer said. "And no one's told him his rights."

The chief looked abruptly at the officer, then back at me. "Then let's get him locked up." The slightest trace of a smile stretched his lips.

I'd yet to say a word. Even though I knew it was righteous, I wasn't about to admit shooting Dragos. Not yet. I wondered if Jerry would personally explain the Fifth Amendment to me.

He stepped to the side while the officers walked me slowly past Dragos's body. I caught a glimpse of Juanita, still at the side of her desk. She was weeping and being tended to by a female paramedic.

The hallway was filled with more police – uniformed and

detectives in business suits. One detective pushed his way into the office. The officers holding me hurried me down the hall toward an elevator. I heard footsteps quickly approaching from behind, and we stopped and turned around. Chief Rhodes stood directly behind us. He stepped up to me, his face inches from mine.

"How come you didn't call me?" he asked in a barely audible voice.

The officers' eyes widened. As though on cue, they both loosened their grip on my arms.

"I was busy," I said back, in an equally low volume.

"When you didn't answer your phone I called in the cavalry. You were lucky."

"See how God works?"

He rolled his eyes. "Yeah. I don't get it. Some people get to live, no matter what."

The officers' eyes grew even wider. Their lips parted while their jaws dropped. They loosened their grip on me even more.

I straightened and shrugged my body into alignment. "So, did you figure everything out?"

The chief continued the bizarre encounter. "Yeah. You want to hear?" Without waiting for my response, he said, "Dragos is dead-bang for Marilyn Chase, and we're close to making him for L.C. Veasley." He nodded his head in the direction of Juanita's office. "Although now we don't have to make the case."

I nodded.

"Looks like your prison informer – Four Dead? – steered you right."

Both officers turned away in a transparent attempt to avoid listening. It didn't matter, the whole story would be known by everyone in the department – everyone in the city – before the day was over.

"So then *I'm* the one who figured everything out."

He knit his brow. "Sometimes it's hard to like you."

He pushed my back against the wall and signaled the officers to leave. They slowly walked away. I could almost see dark clouds of disgust sprinkled with question marks hovering over them.

He turned me around and removed the handcuffs. I rubbed my

wrists.

At that moment the paramedics walked through Juanita's office door and into the hallway, carrying their first aid kits and conspicuously not wheeling a gurney with a body on it. They moved through a gauntlet of officers, some of whom spoke to them in hushed voices. The paramedics kept shaking their heads. One could feel the tension leave the atmosphere. Dead people take the sense of urgency with them.

I nodded in the direction of Juanita's office. "What about the Jones shooting and the killer in the ninja suit?"

"The man in the ninja suit," the chief said without emotion. "Interesting."

He was going to make me work for it. "Now that we've both babbled in riddles, please explain."

He looked at me, a strange, satisfied looking glow around his otherwise expressionless face. He looked toward Juanita's office, and said, "The ninja suit killer is still in that room."

"You mean Dragos? That's the way I'd figured it, until . . ."

He raised a hand and smiled. "Ray-Ray came into the Detective Bureau a few hours ago—"

"He *did*? What's he saying? What's goin' on?"

Rhodes gave me a disapproving look. I stopped.

"Let me explain," he said. "Okay?" He waited, a beat too long, enjoying my angst, relishing his I-know-something-you-don't-know power over me. The way he'd always done, whenever he could.

He continued. "Roniece called Ray-Ray yesterday to warn that Dragos knew about him, and figured Ray-Ray knew things that could hurt him. Dragos made it clear to Roniece he wanted to kill Ray-Ray. Ray-Ray immediately went underground. As you can tell, he and Will Tandy have been having a nice chat."

I tried to speak, but he raised his forefinger, to stop me.

"Our guys knocked on some doors around Colette's house on North 14th Street, and we know that Dragos went there last night and spirited Roniece away."

"He dragged her around, making her help look for Ray-Ray."

"Right."

"We're gonna go through this step-by-step, I see. Coppers do that when they're proud of their work."

The chief laughed, but said nothing.

"Okay, by the numbers then," I said sarcastically, "how did Dragos find Roniece?"

"Well, working at City Hall he had access to every damn information base in the city, besides law enforcement ones. He was a helluva resourceful detective."

"Right. So how did he find her, goddammit?"

"He learned where her mother and L.C. lived, then kept checking both houses 'til he saw Roniece leave L.C.'s. He followed her to the house on North 14th Street, and waited 'til the time was right. Neighbors from all three places were watching and told us all about it this morning."

"Oh. He found her through old-fashioned police work. Resourceful, indeed."

A detective and a uniformed officer emerged from the office, with Roniece walking between them. Her face had darkened. Her eyes were puffy and circled in black, as though ring shaped ink stamps had been pressed onto her face.

The chief turned to look at her, then looked back at me. "The ninja killer has just left the room." He motioned toward the officers leading Roniece away with his thumb for them to move faster with her.

At that moment I saw Roniece's hands cuffed behind her back. Damn! Not until Dragos had started goading her about the murders did I even come close to figuring her for it. And even then it seemed unbelievable – even more unbelievable than a paragon of virtue like a cop being responsible. But how could I have known? It had been natural to assume that Roniece was *running from* a killer, being a woman in the drug world, and all.

"Roniece planned it, then did it," the chief said. "Ray-Ray's story is that she'd heard Earl Jones was threatening to kill her, and she acted first. Apparently, she'd become the go-between for Dragos and Jones. Something bad happened and Jones wanted her dead."

Bitches always fuck up, I recalled Four Dead saying the first time I talked to him. In the macho world of drug dealing, how could things be any different?

"Ray-Ray'd had his own falling out with Jones," the chief said. "And Roniece recruited him to help her – there's something about promising him money and dope. He got her a cold Uzi from the streets and a warm ninja suit from a law enforcement supply store. The burglary of that store was still on file, uncleared."

"Gonna overlook it?" I asked, referring to the burglary.

"We may find mitigating circumstances in Ray-Ray's favor."

"Sounds reasonable. But back to Four Dead – he was Roniece's bitch boy, and he thought he was being a look-out for Jones."

The chief smiled. "That's what Four Dead – Reggie Thackery, as I prefer – had been led to believe, but Roniece tried playing double-cross by framing him as an accomplice in the Jones murder.

"We don't think Thackery ever knew Roniece did the shooting. And Roniece didn't know her friend Kim Artic and the others besides Jones were in the car. She just stepped out banging away."

"Where was Ray-Ray?"

"Claims he wasn't there, that Roniece acted alone."

"Sounds plausible," I said, rolling my eyes. After a moment I asked, "And Dragos? Where exactly does he fit in?"

"Some things we can only guess. It seems like Dragos didn't know about Ray-Ray back then. He may have suspected that Roniece was involved in the ambush, but we can't be sure. He got his ass transferred out of Narcotics pronto, and City Hall looked like a perfect new home."

"He'd made himself into a charwoman," I said. "And everybody on the police force knew it. But hey, he could hide and make good overtime. Pride goeth fast when you're looking at a couple decades in jail."

"Exactly. He played it smart."

"What happened in Thackery's shooting case?"

"Of course, the frame-up of Reggie Thackery for Jones's killing didn't work. Ray-Ray admits being with Jones's guys when they tried" – he made closed quotes with his fingers – "taking revenge on Four Dead two weeks later.

"Ray-Ray'd remained on their good side, even after Jones ran him off. You know how street gangs can be a can of worms that way. Anyway, Ray-Ray's claiming he didn't know his homeys were gonna shoot Thackery, and he ran when it started going down."

"And I'm sure you're gonna believe that, as long as he testifies against Roniece, and gives whatever information he can against Dragos."

"Ain't it great to believe whatever you want to believe?"

I looked around. News reporters had already arrived, some accompanied by video crews. They'd have juicy shots, with Dragos still lying dead in Juanita's office. Many of the officers in the hallway stared unabashedly in the chief's and my direction.

I recalled my imaginary portrait, littered with all my characters, how I hadn't wanted to see anyone else dead. I hadn't gotten my way, but seeing in my mind's eye Vince Dragos lying in the dead zone of the picture didn't bother me.

"Where did Roniece get the ninja suit idea?" I asked.

"Ray-Ray says Dragos mentioned to her how cops using ninja suits and masks can get away with a lot of stuff. Of course, people from the inner city already believe that. She decided to give it a try, figuring that any witnesses would make her for a man. Again, people in that neighborhood would be easily convinced it really *was* a cop in a ninja suit, if that tale were ever spun."

And then Roniece did the murderer thing – she ran scared for two years.

"There's poetic justice somewhere in all this, I'd say."

"It's a complicated poem. That's it on a thumbnail, as I've always said. Oh, one more thing. Thanks for getting the ball rolling, and thanks for dealing with Mr. Dragos. Makes it easier for us."

"Easy for me, too, I'm sure. Will I get my gun back?"

He winked. "If the D.A. decides not to charge you with murder and the coroner's inquest concurs."

"Right. That'll be the easy part."

I looked past him, across the hall. Two detectives walked Roniece into an elevator, and the door slowly slid closed.

Juanita came out of the room, the female paramedic still assisting her. Juanita glanced around and saw me. We exchanged knowing looks. I couldn't wait to get together with her.

"Hey," the chief yelled while turning toward the gaggle of cops. Everyone's head turned toward him.

He pointed at the officers who'd taken me into custody and motioned for them to return. They both looked at my un-handcuffed hands, their faces registering surprise and suspicion.

"Take Mr. Blanchard to the Detective Bureau," the chief said. "Someone there'll interview him."

The now stone-faced officers immediately marched me off.

"Don't look so glum, fellas," I said. "Think of all the paperwork you're getting out of."

Jerry called after me, "Anything you need, you let me know."

We stopped, and I turned around to face him. I affected a drawn-out pause, put on a scrutinizing look. "Well, bitch boy Four Dead – I mean Reginald Thackery – is doing big prison time for a murder that really wasn't so much a 'murder,' if you get my meaning. He's whacked, and he'll always need supervision, but it sounds like Ray-Ray may help his case."

I looked both ways at the officers beside me. I cupped one hand at the side of my mouth and said in a forced, lowered voice, "Maybe someone can take it up with the D.A."

Rob Riley, author of *Portrait of Murder*

Rob Riley lives with his wife, Mary Lynne, in southeastern Wisconsin. He spent thirty-two years as a Milwaukee police officer: seven years doing undercover narcotics investigations and twenty-two years as a major crimes detective. Writing and reading have been lifelong passions, and he began by writing short stories more than thirty years ago. Of course, police work provided both the inspiration and insight for his PI mystery novel, *Portrait Of Murder*. Two additional novels in a series that features his main character, Private Investigator Jack Blanchard, have been completed. The author may be contacted at rob.riley101@yahoo.com

Author photograph © Mary Lynne Riley

CPSIA information can be obtained at www.ICGtesting.com
Printed in the USA
LVOW091908100612

285469LV00003B/62/P